She saw him the second he walked into the cafeteria.

She sat up straighter, smiled as his eyes met hers, lighting up in joy. Not for the first time, she wished that they were something more than what they were. She had not come here expecting to ~~~~ tangled up in the li~~~~ ~~~~ she was.

And when she ha~~~~ ~~~~at life with him wou~~~~ happy scenes in h~~~~ ~~~~king walks together. Walking along the beach, dogs running around their feet. Walking hand in hand, the wind blowing her hair everywhere, so that when he went to kiss her, he would have to tuck her hair behind her ears to see her face, touch her face and gently press his lips to hers. How it would feel to be just his. Truly his.

An unachievable dream, which just made it hurt even more.

Dear Reader,

I've always wanted to set a story on a small island, because I live on one, too! Down here on the south coast, Hayling is next to Thorney Island. You can walk around the perimeter, but that's all, as it's mostly an army base. However, I loved the name and thought it would be a good idea to create my Thorney Island up in the waters around Scotland and put at the heart of it a cottage hospital, where the doctors do many wonderful things.

But who to put there? Adam came to me first and then Jess, both of them troubled by the traumas of their past. It seemed only fair to give them a happy-ever-after.

I hope you love them—and Thorney—as much as I do!

Love,

Louisa xxx

RISKING HER HEART ON THE TRAUMA DOC

LOUISA HEATON

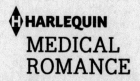

MEDICAL
ROMANCE

HARLEQUIN®
MEDICAL ROMANCE™

Recycling programs
for this product may
not exist in your area.

ISBN-13: 978-1-335-40424-4

Risking Her Heart on the Trauma Doc

This edition published by arrangement with Harlequin Books S.A.

For questions and comments about the quality of this book, please contact us at CustomerService@Harlequin.com.

Harlequin Enterprises ULC
22 Adelaide St. West, 40th Floor
Toronto, Ontario M5H 4E3, Canada
www.Harlequin.com

Printed in U.S.A.

Louisa Heaton lives on Hayling Island, Hampshire, with her husband, four children and a small zoo. She has worked in various roles in the health industry—most recently four years as a community first responder, answering 999 calls. When not writing, Louisa enjoys other creative pursuits, including reading, quilting and patchwork—usually instead of the things she *ought* to be doing!

Books by Louisa Heaton

Harlequin Medical Romance

Visit the Author Profile page at Harlequin.com.

To Mary, my sister, my friend xxx

CHAPTER ONE

JESS KNEW SHE'D made the right decision to come back. Standing at the front of the ferry as it chugged its way towards Thorney Island, she felt the cool breeze blowing through her hair, heard the noisy gulls circling overhead.

Thorney Island looked exactly as she remembered. Only smaller. She'd been brought here as a child by her father. Their annual holiday—one week away in a caravan, year after year, without fail. Until she'd got old enough to want something more.

The bustling harbour was filled with boats of all shapes and sizes: trawlers, dredgers, fishing boats and the occasional pleasure cruiser. It was as if she had only left yesterday, and the aroma in the air of brine and fish was just so familiar, so filled with happy memories, that it almost took her breath away.

She'd missed this, and it was something

she'd never expected to feel—this *longing*. This *grief*. But of course it would remind her of the happy times she'd had here with her father. She should have expected it. Because remembering that happiness simply served to remind her of what she had lost.

The ferry slowed as it came into port, drifting in on the tide. She heard the harbour master and the others calling to one another in their thick Scottish accents and she smiled before she hurried back to get into her car, ready to drive off when they finally docked.

The waterfront looked the same—as if the island had been trapped in time from the second she'd left to this moment she was in now. She thought briefly about stopping to pop into the Harbour Café, to grab a coffee and a bite to eat, but she knew it would be busy, as it always was, and she was keen to get to the estate agents to pick up the key for her temporary rental property.

She'd have the rest of the day to settle in, and then tomorrow she would start work under her new boss, Dr Jack Campbell, who seemed to be a really nice man.

He'd interviewed her on the telephone and in a video call online, as she'd been unable to make it over to the island. He reminded her of her own father. They'd have been the same generation as each other and, with his silver hair and his twinkling blue eyes and his nice smile, Jack had made her feel very comfortable indeed.

She imagined that working for him at the island's cottage hospital would be interesting and educational, considering how broad the work requirements were. And he'd really liked it that she was already familiar with the island as apparently he'd had trouble trying to fill the post—candidates had been turning it down as there wasn't much opportunity to specialise, and most doctors were looking for their next step up the long ladder of success, rather than a small hospital.

The estate agency she was looking for was a little bit inland from the harbourfront, and she drove away from the waterside and found a small parking area behind the first street of shops. She parked, and pushed open the door of Wainwright's Estate Agency, hearing a bell ringing merrily above her head as she walked in.

There were three desks all in a line, and behind each one sat an agent dressed in a grey suit. Over the left breast pocket of their jackets, they each wore a name tag. Two of the agents were on the phone, so she walked over to the female agent who seemed free and glanced at her badge: *Moira*.

'Good morning, can I help you?' Moira smiled, all white teeth and thick-lashed eyes.

'Hello. I'm Dr Jessica Young and I've rented a flat on Haven Road. I was told I could collect the key here.'

'Okay. Do you know who you were dealing with?'

'Adrian.'

'Ah. He's not here today, but I can certainly help you. Have you brought your documents and ID?'

Jess delved into her bag to bring out all that was needed, and after a few moments of checking, she was passed a key with a label hanging from it.

'There's a map in the documentation, but Haven Road isn't far. I can direct you, if you'd like?'

'That's okay. I think I know where it is. It's that long road that runs towards the hospital, isn't it?'

Moira nodded. 'Aye, it is. Well, I hope you're happy there. Any problems, you'll need to contact your landlord. His details are in the pack.'

'Thanks.'

Jess headed back outside and took a brief moment to suck in the briny sea air just one more time before heading inland.

Fresh air and a fresh start was everything her own doctor had prescribed.

'You must be Dr Young—Jessica, isn't it?' asked the bespectacled, perfectly coiffed lady.

'Call me Jess.' She reached out her hand for the older woman to shake.

'Call me Judy. I'm Jack's wife. Also his receptionist and assistant extraordinaire.' She smiled. 'Did you have a calm crossing on the ferry?'

'Very calm, thank you.'

Jess liked Judy. She had the look of a stern librarian, with her glasses attached to a colourful chain around her neck.

'I'm afraid Jack has had to go out on a call, so he's not here to meet you as he planned.' Judy came out from behind her desk and indicated that Jess should follow her. 'Can I get you a cup of tea?'

'Oh, I'm fine, thank you.'

Judy escorted her towards a door that bore a plaque stating *Dr Jack W Campbell, Clinical Lead.*

'He's left a few things you'll need today, so let's get those.'

Jess waited as Judy searched Jack's desk, opening drawers and rummaging, and let her eyes scan the room. It was stylishly decorated, and had some added touches that Jess assumed had been made by Dr Campbell's wife. Some beautiful pot plants that she couldn't name. A sofa to one side of the room, beautifully arranged with some modern cushions, a piece of cross-stitch on the wall, of a busy harbourside filled with boats, and a windowsill filled to the brim with family photos in elegant silver frames.

They all seemed to be of the same person. A little boy growing into the man he appeared to be now. Handsome, too. One photo showed him stood in his university gown holding a scroll, a beaming smile upon his face. And to the side was a picture of the same young man kneeling down with a group of kids, all smiling towards the camera as a hot sun beamed down upon them.

Where was that? Egypt? Somewhere in Africa?

Another showed the man standing in the midst of a jungle, his face turned up to the heavens as it rained, his hands stretched out as if he was grateful for the rain.

'Settled in all right?' asked Judy.

'Yes, I have. I must thank your husband for the recommendation. The flat's a good size.'

'In good condition, too. Our son lives in the same building, so he did us all a favour by giving us his landlord's contact details.'

Their son lived in her building? She smiled, suddenly nervous.

'Ah! Found it!' Judy brandished a file full of paperwork and a temporary ID card on a lanyard with her name on it. 'You can use this until we get your photo taken. It's great to meet you at last. Jack had no doubt about you at all during the interview, but it's always better to meet someone in person, don't you think?'

Jess nodded. 'Absolutely.'

'Okay! So, we'll go through a few house-keeping bits and pieces and then we'll get you started. Adam's all ready to get you up and running.'

She frowned. 'Adam?'

'The other Dr Campbell.' She pointed at the framed photos with pride. 'He's been working abroad, but he's been back with us for just over a year now.'

'I thought I'd be working with Jack,' said Jess, her gaze lingering on the most prominent photo.

Adam was exactly the type of good-looking man that she'd be attracted to.

And she didn't need that sort of complication.

CHAPTER TWO

ADAM SAT IN a curtained-off cubicle, attending to a fisherman who'd got a nasty cut on his hand that needed stitching.

John McAllister had caught his hand whilst out on his latest fishing trip, and had bound it with a dirty used tea towel that had been in the boat's galley. Adam had had to clean it out, rinse the wound with saline and give him a tetanus shot, just to be on the safe side. Now he had his suturing kit out.

He had just tied the first stitch when he heard his mother's voice coming down the corridor, and turned to greet her as the curtains behind him swished open.

But Adam's voice caught in his throat when he spied the stunning young woman standing behind his mother. *Wow.* She was incredibly beautiful! And she'd totally taken his breath away. He actually forgot to breathe for a moment, until his burning lungs forced him to snap out of his trance.

He turned back to his patient and snipped the ends off that first stitch, in a state of disbelief that he'd reacted in such a way.

'Adam, sorry to interrupt you whilst you're working, but this is the new doctor your father was telling you about—Dr Young.'

Adam put down his instruments carefully, trying very hard not to show that his hands weren't in his complete control, and gave his mum his full attention. He liked working for his father. Even though it was different from the way he'd thought it would be and his father didn't let him get away with anything. Not that he tried!

Jack Campbell ran the Thorney Island cottage hospital with a firm hand, ensuring their patients all received top-quality care at every point of contact. Adam didn't get any preferential treatment working for his father, which was what he'd been worried about when he'd first come here, after working abroad for so long with International Health. He'd not wanted the other staff to think that his father treated him differently, and because of that he had been working doubly hard, taking on extra hours and working double shifts whenever it was needed without complaint.

'I'd shake your hand, but…' But he was in the middle of a procedure. He knew she'd understand. Besides, he wasn't sure he wanted to make any physical contact with her.

He tried his hardest not to look at Dr Young again, because she was somehow making him nervous, his body reacting to her in ways he'd not expected.

For such a long time now he'd stopped noticing women in that way, and he'd been totally fine with it. He didn't need complications at work. He certainly didn't need complications in his private life. For a long time women had just been friends and colleagues to him. He liked them, and enjoyed their company, but he had shut off his carefully guarded heart for over a year now and he'd been quite happy that the wall around it was unassailable.

Until now.

This Dr Young—maybe unwittingly—had almost breached his defences. She might not be aware of it, but he certainly was. It was a wobble—and not one he'd been prepared for.

His mother smiled and patted him on the shoulder, as she often did.

'You remember we told you about Dr Young a couple of months ago? You agreed to help show her around the place...work with her until she's up and running and feels confident. Well, I've brought you your apprentice! Not that she's an *actual* apprentice. Dr Young here is perfectly qualified. But she'll benefit from your experience and guidance.'

His mother turned to Dr Young.

'Adam has been working here for just over a year now, but before that he worked overseas in all manner of places! Madagascar, the Congo, Syria, Afghanistan...you name it, he's probably got the fridge magnet.'

She smiled, turning back to him.

'You can teach Dr Young all our procedures, and how we do things—if you could work together for the next few weeks, just until she's got the hang of everything? Your dad would do it himself, but he spends so much time on administration these days I think the only thing Dr Young would learn from him is how bad he is at typing. Is that okay?'

She smiled her motherly smile and Adam knew he couldn't back out of his promise. If he was anything, he was a man of his word.

Adam risked a glance at the new doctor. He

couldn't help it. It was almost as if his brain wanted to confirm that she was, in fact, as devastatingly beautiful as he'd first supposed.

What he saw was a woman who clearly had no idea of her own beauty or her effect on men. Even his previously talkative patient had been struck dumb. Dr Young looked studious behind those black-rimmed glasses, but she also appeared keen to seem amiable. Her smile was broad, and it had the crazy ability to make his heart pound faster than it had ever done before—and he'd been in life-or-death situations more than once.

His body was betraying him. It wasn't meant to do what it was doing. He tried to take in a long, slow breath to calm it down.

'Hello. Nice to meet you,' she said.

She had a very fine accent. English, with a hint of Scottish twang. Very nice.

Fighting to regain some control, he nodded quickly and smiled at his mother. He couldn't show her how he was feeling. He didn't need his mother thinking she was Cupid again. The amount of times she had tried to set him up with someone since he'd returned… He'd had to tell her that he wasn't interested in any of that. Not yet.

His mum had backed off, but he could see

that familiar gleam in her eyes. He knew she wanted him to settle down and give her grandchildren to spoil, the way her friends spoilt theirs. But that wasn't on the cards for him. Not any more. Not since Anoush.

He'd thought he'd marry her. That she was his future and they would have a life in Dubai, or somewhere, but then it had all gone terribly wrong.

Now, after that he didn't see that type of future for himself. So this feeling of attraction, or lust, or whatever was happening right now, could damn well disappear—because nothing would ever happen.

'That's fine with me. As long as it's okay with Dr Young?'

She smiled at him, blushed slightly, and he felt as if someone had punched him in the gut.

'Jess.'

Jess.

She gave him a brief nod, and seemed pleased about the situation. He had the idea that the quicker she got used to the place—where everything was and the procedures they followed—the quicker he could work on his own again, get that distance back and rebuild his wall. Which was something he clearly needed to do. With every second he spent with her, he could feel his willpower crumbling away.

'Good. Well, I'll leave you to it then. Adam, you'll meet us for lunch?' his mum asked.

'Aye.'

They both watched Judy walk away, and then Jess pulled across the cubicle's curtain and introduced herself to John McAllister, who shook her hand.

'Nasty cut you've got there,' she said, peering closer.

When she leant in Adam could smell her perfume. It wasn't anything overpowering, but light and fresh, and it did strange things to his senses.

'Aye. Did it this morning, hauling in the latest catch.'

'Crab? Cod?'

'Mackerel. Normally we get a good haul this time of year. Usually come back with a full load. But we had to cut it short today, because of this.'

'Must be nice to be out on the boat… How big is your crew?'

'Just the three of us.'

Adam began to feel like a spare part. How

had she managed to make him feel this way?
He'd been in complete control of this situation to start with, but now that Jess was
there, and his patient was also falling under
her spell, he began to feel a little irritated.

Angry with himself—for this was his problem, not hers—he picked up his instruments
once again and began suturing as Jess and
his patient talked.

Looking on the bright side, perhaps this
wouldn't be so bad at all. Jess could talk to
the patients whilst he got on with the job at
hand and then maybe he could get away with
not having to talk to her. Or the patients! The
less interaction the better. He could be monosyllabic—or just grunt.

*Who are you kidding? You could never be
that rude.*

Besides, she seemed just as nervous as he
was. He could hear it in her voice. In the
slight quaver in her throat. Probably just first-
day nerves. She'd be fine in a few days.

*And so will I. It was just a shock, that's all.
My foundations were...challenged.*

At least that was what he tried to tell himself, but he could feel that his hands were
sweating like mad in the gloves, and he
couldn't quite tie the stitches correctly. He

kept fumbling, taking deep breaths, trying to steady himself.

He knew what to do—had done this *thousands* of times! He'd sutured with a steady hand under the threat of bullets before. But for some reason—probably because Jess was looking over his shoulder—he was now having difficulties.

When the next stitch failed to tie, he put down his instruments and stretched out his fingers, as if they were cramped.

'Everything all right?' she asked.

Even though she hadn't said anything derogatory he felt belittled—and embarrassed that he couldn't tie a simple suture. He was a trauma doctor. He should be able to do this blindfold.

'I'm fine!' he replied, a little more aggressively than he liked.

'I'd be happy to take over if you'd like a break. Your mum said you'd done one shift already…'

Adam looked at his patient. He didn't seem to mind who did the stitches as long as it got done. The man had work to do and no doubt wanted to get back to his boat. And Adam didn't want his pride to get in the way.

'No, it's okay. It was just a little cramping,

that's all. I can do it. You can observe.' He regretted the suggestion as soon as he'd made it when she stepped closer to him and leaned in and his body reacted keenly to her presence.

What the hell was happening?

He picked up his instruments once again and concentrated so hard anyone would have thought he was a student again, being observed in an OSCE. That was an Objective Structured Clinical Examination, which often used to test clinical skill performances and competencies in medical training. Students would be set a series of tests and be examined by one or two examiners in a real or simulated situation.

He'd always hated that sort of thing—being observed so intently, knowing that the observer was looking for mistakes. And he definitely didn't want to make a mistake in front of Dr Jess Young. It was important to him that she saw him as the confident and knowledgeable doctor that he was.

This time he made the stitch, and the next one, and the next. He slowly let out a pent-up breath and concentrated hard until the suturing was done. He smiled at John as he finished and dressed the wound, then gave him aftercare instructions.

Once he was done, he dismissed him, cleared up his equipment and glanced at Jess. 'Right, I just need to write this up.'

'Okay.' She followed him over to the doctors' computer terminal and sat down beside him. 'I really like your parents.'

He smiled. 'Thanks.'

'Do you find it weird, having your dad as your boss?'

'I did a little, at first. But I find it easy to separate the two. When we're at work we're colleagues and good friends, respectful of each other. When we're at home we're more relaxed and like family.'

'I like your mum, especially. Have your parents always worked together?'

'Mum was a nurse when Dad began here as a doctor. She gave up nursing because of ill health, but sort of took over being Dad's secretary and the hospital receptionist.'

'I hope she's okay now?'

He nodded and glanced at her curiously. He'd known she was beautiful from about a metre away, but up close he saw she had skin like porcelain and brown eyes tinted with flecks of honey-gold. And her mouth, her lips...

I'll probably dream about that mouth...

Her smile lit up her entire face and he could have admired it all day. But then he became aware that he was probably staring a little bit too much and felt self-conscious.

Thankfully, she was the one to break the awkwardness. 'So, what sort of patients do you normally get here? I don't remember the hospital being this small.'

'You've been here before?'

'My father used to bring us to Thorney every year for a week's holiday. I can remember driving past this place and thinking it was huge.' She laughed.

'It's a cottage hospital. We don't do anything overly complicated here. Anything that requires major surgery gets sent to the mainland. We have a midwife here, a gerontologist and a paediatrician, and a primary care clinic. I don't know what you're used to, or if you've worked in a big city. We get scrapes and cuts, the occasional broken bone, one or two urgent resus cases. Typical stuff.'

'You enjoy it after working abroad? That must have been exciting?'

'Very much so. But I enjoy making a difference here.'

Adam typed in his pass code. The screen

sprang into life and he began typing in John McAllister's treatment details.

He became acutely aware of how close she was. Normally he would sit here and be just as close to other members of staff and it never mattered. But with Jess it was different. His pulse rate had accelerated and he felt hot and nervous, his fingers skipping over the keys and making mistakes that he had to delete, bashing the delete key with an irritation he didn't want to feel. He could feel her eyes upon him and almost couldn't stand it.

'What about you? Where have you worked before? Will a cottage hospital on a tiny island be enough for you?'

Jess nodded. 'Absolutely. I was working in a big hospital in Nairn, in A&E mostly, but things happen in life that make you reconsider what you're doing with it. After I lost my father I took stock of my life and knew I needed something with a more sedate pace. I remembered this place and when a vacancy came up, I knew I had to fill it.'

But Adam saw something in her eyes as she talked that intrigued him. It was as if she was telling him the truth but keeping out some parts that she didn't want to share with him.

He looked at her, considering her. 'So, you're focused?'

'I am. And ready for what comes next.'

'Well, you'll get a wide variety here. Lots of the staff have multiple roles. It's never boring.'

'That's good. I'm not after boring, and I'm not after easy. I want you to push me hard. Help further my education and understanding.'

'I can do that.'

'What about you? What made you choose to come back here and not stay abroad?'

He shrugged his shoulders and tried to act as if his decision to work here hadn't been a big deal at all. 'It was time to come home. I'd been away for too long and I wanted to work with the people I lived with. I like the continuity of care in the community we have here on the island. There are roughly twenty thousand people on Thorney, and they look after each other. It's close-knit and I like that. It's family.'

'And you needed to be back with family? I get that. It's the most important thing, isn't it?'

She sounded sad. And wistful. It made him wonder what her sadness was. She'd mentioned losing her father, and Adam couldn't imagine losing his. It would rock his world when that terrible day came. Did she know how strong she was, carrying on with that kind of heartache? He admired her.

'Yes. It is,' he said.

And I'm staring again.

He turned away. 'I guess you don't have a GP yet?'

She shook her head. 'No. I'll have to register with someone now that I'm living over here.'

He smiled. 'I can give you a few names of the doctors who still have places on their lists.'

'Thank you. That's very kind of you.'

Was it, though? He felt as if he'd done nothing but judge and assess her since they'd met. She seemed sweet and kind, had been good with the one patient he'd watched her interact with. She was easy to talk to, and clearly intelligent, and it was hardly *her* fault that his body was reacting to her in ways he didn't want or need.

Showing her a little kindness was all he could do.

But when you recognised something in yourself, you could easily see it in others. And he'd seen how she'd looked away from him when she'd spoken about coming here for the job. Something had hurt her apart from the death of her father. It still hurt her. But what business was it of his? She didn't have to tell him anything and nor did he want to know.

Keep her at arm's length.

'I've noticed you have a limp. Can I ask what happened?' Her cheeks flushed as she asked the question, as if she was not sure he would answer her.

'Oh…car accident. It's not a big problem.'

She nodded, smiling, but he could tell she didn't believe him. But she'd done a good thing by asking him that particular question—his walls had gone back up.

He finished off John McAllister's notes and locked down the computer. There was no one else waiting in the walk-in clinic.

'Don't know about you, but I'm ready for some coffee,' he said.

Perhaps a hit of caffeine would refresh him and knock some sense into his disturbed, newly aware body, which was most definitely feeling way too many feels.

So the photos of Adam in Jack's office had been one thing, but the man himself…

Holy moly.

If she'd been able to fan herself she would have—but, no, she'd had to stand there and try to act normal. Try to act as if she hadn't had her legs swept out from under her—because that was how she'd felt.

Adam was *hot*!

Piercing blue eyes... That just-got-of-bed hair that looked as if a comb had never touched it, but had in fact clearly been carefully styled, flopping over his forehead all too casually... Broad, strong shoulders... the sleeves of his blue checked shirt straining over the size of his biceps... A neat, flat waist...

Definitely a ten out of ten in the looks department.

And he was going to be her mentor.

How on earth am I going to be able to work with him every day?

She'd managed to introduce herself without tripping over her tongue, and she hoped she'd also managed to look capable and interested in his patient.

When he'd stood up to take them both over to the doctors' station she'd been aware he was a good few inches taller than her, and estimated he had to be just over six feet in height. His limp was barely there, but she'd noticed that he favoured his right leg over his left, and that the damaged leg didn't seem to have as much ease of movement as the other.

Nerves had got the best of her. It had been inevitable really. With nothing to do with her hands, she'd started asking him questions. The one about his leg had just popped out and she'd cringed inwardly. It was hardly a first day question, was it? She could have waited until she'd known him for a few weeks.

Had she been rude? Had she pried a little bit too far into something that was none of her business?

He'd brushed her off, saying it had been a car accident as if it was nothing—but she'd worked in A&E, and an accident that had managed to damage his leg up near what looked like his hip flexors had to have been considerable. He'd been hurt. Badly. Yet he was brushing it off.

She liked him for that. Some people couldn't wait to tell you all about their ills and what had happened to them—the fact that Adam hadn't, just boosted her estimation of him. Plus, she understood his not wanting to tell her everything. There was plenty *she* was holding back, and she would continue to do so until she absolutely had to reveal it.

A person's secrets were their own.

Whatever was going on with Adam Campbell was absolutely nothing to do with her.

He was a *colleague*. Nothing more. No matter how stunning he looked. No matter what he did to her insides when he looked at her. No matter how he made her legs feel like jelly.

And she would hardly answer any questions he asked her about *her* health, now, would she?

Adam led Jess to the small staff room, where there was a kitchenette in the corner.

Her question had caused his barricades to come up again, for which he was grateful. He had spent the last year or so building them. Trying to close the door on a terrible chapter in his life that he didn't want to think about.

He was just a little testy today because Anoush's birthday was coming up soon, and his damned brain kept interrupting his day-to-day life to remind him of that fact and keep him on edge.

That first birthday without her had been

the most awful day of his life, and he didn't want to have to go through that agony again. He'd managed to hide his suffering from those who knew him here. He'd even booked the day off. But he wasn't going to do that this year.

Last time he'd allowed himself to wallow in his pity and his grief, and he'd drunk more than he should have to try and numb the pain he'd been feeling. It had been the wrong tactic to employ. So this year he was going to take it as just another day and show up to work. If he kept busy—if he made his focus other people, instead of himself—it just might be bearable.

Jess had asked about his leg, but the injury had happened in the ambush and he didn't want to speak of that ever again. He wanted to put it behind him and use his theory for himself to ignore, ignore, ignore. But something about her asking had instantly niggled, and he'd had to say something.

He wasn't ready to share about what had happened in Afghanistan. If he was going to talk to anyone about that it was going to be a therapist, and seeing as there was no therapist at the cottage hospital on Thorney Island he guessed he would have to go to the mainland for that kind of service.

There was probably a counsellor knocking around the hospital—because he couldn't imagine that a hospital caring for twenty thousand people wouldn't at least have *someone* trained in mental health—but he wasn't going to go looking for them. Not now. And probably, if it was left up to him, he'd never do so. He was coping on his own. He didn't need someone poking about in his mind and he certainly didn't need Jess doing so either.

What was it about her that bothered him so? Was it just physical? The way her brown eyes had met his? He'd felt an instant connection. A connection that shouldn't have happened with a perfect stranger. But it had, and he'd been left feeling winded—as if he'd taken a bullet to the lung. His heart had begun to pound, to race, he'd grown hot, and when she'd smiled nervously at him it had all been too much!

She'd looked at him and asked him that question as if she really *cared*. And that was odd because she hardly knew him. Maybe it was just the doctor in her, or something, but there'd been something about the look in her eyes that had told him he needed to get away. Self-preservation.

He didn't need someone caring about him. He didn't need to make strong connections. That was the whole point of coming back to Thorney Island. He wanted the safety of family. Of a world where there were no complicated relationships. Where nothing ever happened. The point wasn't to get involved with anyone apart from his parents, whom he knew would not be able to stop themselves from caring. He didn't need it from anyone else.

'Coffee? Tea?' he asked.

'Tea, please. White, no sugar.'

'Take a seat.'

He ran his hands through his hair as he walked towards the tea-making facilities and took a deep breath, exhaling slowly. He needed to lose the hair trigger. This was Thorney Island, not Kabul. There were no wars here—no landmines, no ambushes. Just the people he'd grown up with. Fishermen, farmers... Run-of-the-mill people who were just getting on with their lives. Just like those people in Afghanistan until war had come.

He had to stop looking for traps—had to stop second-guessing everything. He had to get a hold of himself and tell himself that Jess was not the enemy. She was a junior doctor, here to learn under his tutelage, and once he'd done that job he could set her free to work under her own steam. The quicker he did that, the better.

But he wished his brain would tell his stomach to calm down. It was churning with nerves, and his mouth was dry, and he felt apprehensive about spending time with her.

Come on, mate. You're hardly going to start a relationship with her, are you? Calm the hell down!

He presented her with her drink and she sat opposite him on the blue sofa, her hands cradling the mug, her large brown eyes looking at him with gratitude.

'This is perfect. Thanks.'

'No problem.'

Inwardly he wondered if she realised what kind of effect she was having on him. With those big brown eyes behind her glasses, her shoulder-length wavy hair with its golden highlights, her wide smile… She wore a wedding ring on a chain around her neck. A big ring. A man's? Her father's?

'You…er…you mentioned that your father had died. Do you have any other family?'

Family was important to Adam. It was what had kept him going when he was abroad, knowing that they were back home, rooting for him. He'd frequently video called them when he'd had the chance and it had always felt good to know that he had a soft place to fall. He hoped she had something similar.

'No. Nobody. My mother died when I was really young. I don't even remember her, to be honest—though I do have photos. I don't have any siblings.'

'Only child?'

She sipped her tea and nodded.

'Me, too,' he said. 'No aunts or uncles?'

'Yes. An aunt—my father's sister. But she lives in Vancouver. I've never met her, and she didn't come over for the funeral. They weren't all that close, apparently.'

'So you're making it in the world all on your own?'

Jess smiled. 'I am.'

'And you decided Thorney Island was the place to do that?'

She tilted her head to one side. 'Yes. I have so many fond memories of Thorney…it made perfect sense for me to come back here. It's where I feel closest to my father.'

He heard a wobble in her voice and realised

her father's loss still hurt. But of course it would. She was alone in the world and making her own way. Who was he to judge how she chose to do that?

'Adam, I… I didn't mean to be nosy earlier, asking about your leg. I hope you don't think I was being rude. It kind of popped out, and I want to apologise if I stuck my nose in where it wasn't wanted. I do that… Open my mouth before engaging my brain. Call it my super-power.'

She was babbling, trying to make a joke of it, and he marvelled at her optimism. Even though she'd been through some dark times and was now alone, she wasn't letting it hold her back or colour the way she viewed the world. She seemed determined to be bright and upbeat and perky.

Perhaps he could learn something from that…

He looked at her. 'I wasn't offended. It's just a long story and I try not to think about it.'

'Of course. And you're being very gracious. Thank God you're not one of those evil bosses who lays huge piles of work upon new doctors and consigns them to doing nothing but rectal exams all week!'

She laughed, then looked nervous again, and he couldn't help but laugh, too.

'You never know… I just might.' He smiled back, to show it was just a joke, and for a brief moment he forgot that he was meant to be keeping her at a distance. Forgot that he'd decided to try and have as little interaction with her as possible because of the threat she presented to his emotions.

She brightened up the room and he was enjoying her company. It was a long time since he'd felt that…

But as soon as he realised what was happening he immediately began to bring the shutters back down. He looked down at his drink, suddenly unable to look at her, as if looking at her would somehow make him fall to his doom, or something.

She must have realised he was struggling with something, because she said, 'You've had a long shift. You must be tired, and now you're saddled with me. I'm sorry.'

He gave a small nod. He *was* tired. But not physically. It was emotionally. And she was just so bright and peppy! As if she was full of energy and keen to *do* something—to contribute, to help out.

How many hours had he worked this shift? He couldn't remember. It was often like this. Sometimes he just kept going for hours and hours, and often the days blended into one long shift.

'When did you last eat?' she asked, 'You should try and keep your energy up.'

When *had* he last eaten? He couldn't remember. He had some vague memory of cold pizza?

'Your father left me some paperwork to fill in. It'll take me an hour or two, I should think. Why don't you grab a bite to eat and take a power nap while I do it? I promise I won't deal with any patients without you.'

That did sound good. He was grateful to her. But why was she so nice?

'You wouldn't mind?'

'Course not! Point me in the direction of the hospital cafeteria and I'll bring you back a snack.'

He gave her directions, and a note from his wallet, but by the time she came bounding back to the staff room, armed with a banana, a yoghurt and a chicken salad sandwich he was fast asleep on the sofa, completely ignorant of the way she gently and carefully draped a crocheted blanket over him and stood looking at him, a gentle smile upon her face.

CHAPTER THREE

WHEN ADAM WOKE, he located Jess coming out of the administration offices, clipping her ID card to a lanyard, and told her he'd give her a full tour of Thorney Island cottage hospital. He'd found the food she'd brought him, laid on the coffee table next to him and, feeling ravenous, he'd devoured it in seconds. Now, rejuvenated by the food and the nap, he was raring to go.

They were walking down the long corridor towards the X-ray department when he felt his phone buzz in his pocket with a message. He pulled it out and checked the screen.

Come to dinner tonight. Bring Jess. Mum xxx

He smiled, shaking his head. His mother never stopped trying to set him up.

'Something important?' Jess asked.

He laughed. 'No. It was my mother, inviting you to a family dinner tonight. But of course you don't have to accept. I'm sure you have lots to do and—'

'I'd love to come to dinner. Your parents have been so kind to me, helping me out with everything, it'd be rude to refuse.'

'Right.'

'Unless it's a problem for *you*?'

'No, no, not at all!'

He found himself scrabbling to explain that it didn't matter one iota to him whether or not she came to dinner with his family tonight, but found he couldn't find words at all. Because it did matter. It mattered hugely.

He was trying to keep his interactions with Jess at a minimum, but so far he was failing miserably at the task. He could just imagine what his mother would be like tonight. Making hints. Suggesting he take Jess out and about around the island to show her the sights.

Well, he didn't have to do that, did he? She'd come here as a child. He felt absolutely sure she knew most of them already. Besides, she'd want to settle into her new flat—which was in *his* building, he reminded himself. He'd given his landlord's details to his dad for the new doctor, never expecting for one moment the new doctor would be a woman like Jess.

'No problem at all.' Even to himself, he sounded a little curt. 'I'll text her back and let her know you're coming.'

'Great! I'll look forward to it. I can drive us both home afterwards, can't I? Your mum said we live in the same building.'

Ah. He didn't normally go in cars unless he couldn't help it. He walked, or took buses, or cycled. It only took ten minutes of fast cycling to get from one end of the island to the other.

'You don't have to do that.'

'I'm hardly going to let you *walk* home!'

He grimaced a smile. 'Thanks,' he said, and texted his mother his reply.

Jessica Young was living in the flat above him. How crazy was that? He didn't know how to feel about that right now—and the more he thought about it, *worried* pretty much summed it up.

He continued to walk towards the X-ray department, knowing she was following as he pointed out the waiting area and the protocols they used. But his brain was going crazy at the thoughts of possibly bumping into Jess in the mornings, or having to ask her to turn her music down or to lend him a cup of sugar.

He needed to distract himself. *Work. Think of work.*

'We have a radiologist, but she only works days. Anyone who comes in with a suspected fracture during the night has to go to the mainland. Though once a week she's on twenty-four-hour call.'

'Doesn't that make life awkward?'

He was used to life being awkward—in many ways.

'Sometimes, but what can we do? Besides, most people here are in bed at night. You've got to remember you're in a quiet backwater now, with eighty percent of the population over sixty-five and in bed by ten. This little island of ours is hardly action central.'

'I'm glad to hear it. It's what I want. A quieter way of life with less stress.'

Okay, so maybe he wouldn't have to tell her to turn her music down. He'd heard the yearning in her voice, the wistfulness, the true desire for a quiet life. He'd seen himself what excitement and stress and horror could bring, so he understood the yearning well enough. Well, she would certainly find what she was looking for here.

'I'll show you the rest.'

And he led her past the X-ray department and into the primary care centre where his father occasionally worked.

It didn't take them long to look around the hospital. Adam pointed out the equipment rooms, the wards, sluices. He pointed out the pharmacy and the small pathology department where they ran blood tests.

Jess seemed quite amazed at how compact and efficient the small hospital was, and how some people doubled up in their skills. But it was a place that Adam had come to love, and he hoped that she could tell how much—how proud he was to work here, to be a part of this place, the beating heart of Thorney Island. It was unique, sure. And that made it special.

He couldn't imagine working anywhere else now. And he couldn't believe he'd ever wanted to leave this place, thinking it was boring and unable to hold his attention. But he'd been a young man when he'd left. Eighteen years old when he'd headed to the mainland for university and his medical degree, and the big, wide world that had beckoned.

He'd thought he would find excitement and adventure—and he had. But he'd also found loss, pain and heartbreak. He'd lost a bit of himself that he would never get back.

'Have you decided on a specialty yet?' Adam asked.

She shook her head. 'No, but I've got plenty of time to choose.'

She did. But in his experience most doctors had *some* idea of where they thought they'd end up.

'But right now, if you had to choose, what would you say?'

He was truly curious. He didn't know much about Jess. Perhaps her choice in specialty would tell him a little more about her? Cardiology or neurosurgery would show the ultimate ambition...

She shrugged, still smiling. 'I don't know... obstetrics?'

'The only specialty where you end up with more patients than you started with?'

Jess laughed. 'You probably think I'm being silly—viewing it as something that generally has happy outcomes. But I'm a realist. I know things don't always end that way. Obstetrics may have some of the best highs, but it has the lowest of the lows, too.'

He stopped to look at her. 'Have you worked in a maternity unit yet?'

She nodded. 'Yes. I did a two-month rotation.'

'Good.' He was glad she wasn't viewing it through rose-tinted spectacles. Most of the maternity cases they saw on the island ended happily, but there'd been one or two that hadn't, and he liked to think she'd be prepared for that.

'You said there's a midwife here, but do you have a dedicated obstetrician for the more complicated cases?'

'No, they have to go to the mainland.'

She smiled. 'So perhaps my choice is a good one, then!'

He watched her walk ahead and then caught up with her. 'Perhaps. But you'll get a broad spectrum of experience here. The work is so varied from one day to the next, and I kind of like that—never quite knowing what I'm going to face each day. Am I going to be in primary care? Am I going to be working in the walk-in clinic? Or am I going to be doing minor surgeries?'

'That's why I came here. Your father promised me variety.'

'You'll get it.'

His phone beeped again with another message and he removed it from his pocket, dreading that it would be another message from his mother, perhaps suggesting he pick up some flowers for Jess, or something. But it wasn't. It was from the nurse who answered the calls from Reception.

Adam read the message and raised his eyebrows. 'Looks like your wish might be coming true. We're needed out in the community. A baby on the way! Are you up for that?'

Jess beamed. 'Absolutely! But doesn't the midwife attend these cases?'

'She's on the mainland at the moment. Having a knee operation. Come on.'

They hurried down the corridor towards a room by the main reception desk, where a bag was kept stocked for emergencies such as this. They grabbed everything they thought they would need.

'Shall we take my car?' asked Jess.

He felt immediately uncomfortable, and let out a heavy sigh. 'Sure.'

He hadn't had to go out in the community for a while, and when he did he cycled, carrying his equipment in panniers over the back wheel. He very often got to places faster than cars could. They were often held back by slow traffic, or lights, or frequent roadworks, whereas he could glide on through by using the cycle paths. But he guessed there was no escaping the drive this time.

Somewhere, a woman was waiting for their help. And he couldn't let his own discomfort and fear stop her from getting that.

'Why don't you get the details of where we need to go? Rachel has them. The nurse with the dark ponytail.'

Jess gave a brief nod and hurried off to complete the task.

Adam quickly opened the bag and gave the contents a brief scan, checking to make sure that it was fully stocked. He grabbed a few extra pairs of gloves and was putting them inside just as Jess returned with her car keys and a piece of paper with an address scribbled on it.

'Grainger Lane. Number twenty-four. Do you know it?'

He nodded. His adrenaline was pumping now. This was exactly the sort of thing he dreaded. Being trapped in a car. Being trapped in a car with Jess. But he knew she'd be excited. It was the perfect opportunity to show what she could do. And it would be interesting to watch her—see if she really was cut out for this kind of work.

He'd birthed a few babies here on Thorney, and one or two abroad. It was generally a happy thing to do, leaving you on an endorphin high.

Did Jess need any more endorphins? She already seemed happy enough. Upbeat, always ready with a smile and a kind word… But was there something lurking in the dark behind that happiness? Was she trying hard to mask something she didn't want to talk about?

He had a suspicion it was connected to the death of her father. He'd seen it in her eyes. A distant look. Something he couldn't quite name. Yet.

No. And I won't. Jess Young is none of my business.

I've got plenty of time to choose.

That was what she'd said—but that was the thing, wasn't it? She *didn't* have plenty of time. Her clock was ticking. Every day brought the risk that today would be the day that something would go wrong. That she would start experiencing the symptoms that would mark the beginning of her deterioration.

Of course Adam didn't know that, but it was something *she* was very much aware of.

It was part of the reason her last relationship had broken up.

She and Eddie had been so happy... They'd even started talking about having a baby!

She remembered the dinner she and Eddie had had with her dad, when she'd told him that they were going to start trying. She'd expected her dad to be happy, to give them both a hug and wish them the best of luck. Only he hadn't. He'd looked away, and before he'd looked away she'd seen something on his face that had looked like horror. And fear.

She hadn't understood it, and when he had gone home she'd snuggled into Eddie and cried, upset that her father didn't want to share their joy. Why didn't he want them to try for a baby? Why was the prospect so horrific to him? He wasn't old-fashioned— wasn't one of those people who thought you needed to be married before starting a family—and she'd known her dad certainly didn't dislike Eddie. They'd both got along so well!

And then... And then her dad had died. Taken his own life and left Jess the note that had shattered her world.

A life-limiting disease. Hereditary. Huntington's.

Eddie had been supportive at first—her

absolute rock. Telling her she was fine, but that maybe she ought to get herself tested to see if she would develop it, too. But when the result came back—yes, she did indeed carry the gene, and would suffer from Huntington's too—Eddie had left her, also leaving a note.

The coward couldn't even tell me to my face!

Alone in the world, she'd made a conscious decision that she would not let her diagnosis stop her from being who she wanted to be. She would continue to be a doctor and, although she might not ever get the chance to be an obstetrician, she would enjoy the maternity cases when they came along. That was why she'd been so pleased after talking to Jack. He'd told her that they all mucked in wherever they were needed at the cottage hospital. Primary care, minor surgery... *obstetrics.*

But she'd also known that from then on she would stand on her own. She'd been let down by the two men whom she'd thought loved her as much as she loved them and the disease had destroyed everything. Her relationship with her father, her relationship with Eddie, her future...

She couldn't stand the idea that someone

else would get close enough to watch her lose her functionality. Lose her ability to do simple tasks. It wasn't fair to expect someone to be involved with her romantically and then take her on as a responsibility. To become her carer.

Her father had felt the same way. And although she knew that she would not take the escape route that he had, she knew that loved ones left you when it got complicated. That was what she had learned.

She'd had enough darkness. From now on she was determined only to see the light and the love that was in the world. Even if it was never destined to be hers.

Adam was being very quiet. She kept glancing at him and noticed that he seemed agitated, constantly looking out of the window, his gaze shifting rapidly from one side of the car to the other, as if checking their surroundings. What was he looking for? Clearly it was something. Or was he was trying to distract himself from the fact that he was in a car? He'd said he'd damaged his leg in a car accident…perhaps he was worried?

'I'm a good driver, Adam,' she said.

'I'm pleased to hear it. But even good drivers get taken off the road.'

Wow. Okay. 'I'm being very careful.'

'Good. Just keep your eyes on the road and not on me, please.'

She tried not to take offence. He was nervous. Very, very nervous.

His hands rested in his lap—but perhaps 'rested' was the wrong word? His knuckles were white and his hands held on to each other as if they were a lifeline. That was when he wasn't rubbing the sweat from his palms onto his trousers. What had happened in that accident? What didn't she know?

Jess made herself concentrate on the road and the traffic around them, sticking to the speed limit and being very cautious.

Traffic on the island was generally okay. There were one of two roads that could get jammed up during school drop-off times and rush hour, as people headed to work, or to the ferry to catch the boat to the mainland— there were plenty of people who worked off-island. But right now the roads were good. And, even though there was a woman out there about to become a mother, she would not speed. That mother was relying on them arriving safely.

All Jess knew was what the nurse had told her—that the mother was close to delivering and her husband had not been able to get her into the car.

She liked the sound of this call. It hadn't happened at her old job—usually the midwives were called out and they'd hear all about it in the staff room—but she appreciated going outside of the hospital, working in the community, getting hands-on.

Apparently all the doctors at the hospital did it occasionally, when it was required of them. It was part of the service. And it was a service she would enjoy providing, seeing more of this beautiful island that had always made her so happy.

It crossed Jess's mind that if she couldn't be an obstetrician before time passed and her condition got worse, then maybe she could become a doula. That would still allow her to do the work that she wanted to do without the responsibility of being a medic. She could coach women through labour without actually having to deliver the baby.

She hoped that might work. She hoped that once she was unable to carry on being a doctor she would still have options. Because she couldn't picture just sitting at home, hiding away, waiting to die. It wasn't who she was.

She liked people…she liked helping…she liked *doing.*

'Are you okay?' Jess asked Adam as they stopped at a traffic light.

'I'm fine,' he answered in a clipped tone.

Jess wanted to say that normally when people said *I'm fine* it meant that they were nothing of the sort. That they were just trying to stop the other person from worrying about them. But she wasn't going to push, so she just turned to look at the lights, waiting for them to turn green, before driving on.

Grainger Road wasn't far now. About two minutes away, according to her car's navigation system. She hoped they would get there in time, but knew that babies went at their own pace and nobody else's. And even if they were late, they could still help, making sure that mum and baby were okay and completing the necessary afterbirth checks before returning to the hospital.

'So, how many babies have you delivered before?'

That had to be a safe question for her to ask him. It was a professional question, not personal. And maybe, just maybe, it might take his mind off whatever was bothering him about being in a car.

'A few here. One in a jungle hut and another at a field hospital in Afghanistan.'

She smiled. This was most definitely safer ground. 'And how did those births go?'

'Both mothers and babies were fine. Though it was touch and go with the first. The baby was too big for a vaginal delivery and we had to perform an episiotomy to get the baby out. It was huge. Ten pounds.'

'Wow. That beats mine. The largest baby I ever delivered was just over nine pounds.'

Jess pulled up in front of the house, and before they'd even got their seat belts off a man who must be the baby's father came running out to greet them.

'Are you the doctors?'

'We are. I'm Dr Young and this is Dr Campbell.' They both showed the ID badges hanging round their necks. 'How's she doing?'

'She wants to push. I've been trying to get her out of the bath, but she says she can't move.'

'And her name is…?'

'Sarah. Sarah Crosby. And I'm Joe. Her husband.'

Adam was already out of the car carrying the kit bag as she followed Joe down the front path towards the house. It was a neat little home, semi-detached, with a climbing jasmine plant creeping over a trellis arch that marked the front door.

'Does Sarah have any medical issues that we need to know about?'

Joe pushed open the front door. 'No, she's healthy as a horse.'

'And is this your first baby?'

Joe grinned. 'Yes. She's this way.'

He led them up the stairs and they could hear a woman's groans and heavy breathing before they even made it to the bathroom.

Jess quickly assessed the situation. Sarah was kneeling over the edge of the bath, in water up to her waist. She was breathing heavily, her brow damp with sweat from her exertions.

Jess knelt down quickly and took Sarah's hands in her own. 'Hey, Sarah. My name's Jess and this is Adam. We're both doctors and we're here to help, okay? Tell me how you're feeling right now.'

Beside her, Adam put down the bag and began to get out the equipment that they might need.

'I need to start pushing. I've been trying not to, but sometimes I can't help it. The contractions are coming thick and fast!' Sarah cried.

'How long are your contractions lasting?'

Behind her, Joe answered. 'They're over a minute long and she seems to have only about thirty seconds between each one.'

Adam took over. 'That sounds about right. I'm just going to wash my hands, put on some gloves, and then I'm going to check on you, Sarah, okay? That means I'm going to have to do an internal examination, just to check your dilation. In the meantime, if you have another contraction, try not to push—just breathe through it. Can you do that for me?'

Jess could feel her heart beginning to pound with the adrenaline coursing through her system. Joe's excitement was in clear evidence too, and Sarah was clearly 'in the zone'.

This could have been me. If it wasn't for the Huntington's...if it wasn't for Eddie leaving...this could have been me.

She tried not to think too hard about that. The loss of her imagined future family was too much to bear. It was much easier to suppress it.

'Oh, God, here comes another one!' Sarah

squeezed her eyes shut and began to groan, breathing in fits and starts.

'Try and keep your breathing nice and steady. That's it…in and out, in and out.'

Adam quickly washed his hands in the sink and donned a pair of gloves. The contraction was over by the time he'd finished, and he quickly performed an examination of Sarah's cervix, reaching around her as she knelt in the bathtub.

'Okay, that's perfect. You're ten centimetres, and baby's low, so on the next contraction you can begin to push. When the contraction comes, I want you to take a deep breath and then push out through your bottom. I want you to do that at least three times with each contraction, okay?'

'Yeah, I can do that. Can I have a drink of water?'

Her husband passed her a glass with a straw and she sucked on it hungrily before passing it back.

'Thanks.'

Adam soaked a clean face flannel under the cold tap and rinsed it out before handing it to Joe. 'You might want to use this.' He settled on the floor and looked at Sarah again. 'I think I recognise you.'

Sarah looked at him curiously, tucking her hair behind the ear. 'Adam… Right. I think you were in the year above me at school. You were in that play, weren't you?'

Adam smiled. 'I was in a few.'

'You were a very funny vampire—oh, heck, here comes another!'

Adam coached Sarah through her pushing, telling her when to take another breath and counting out as she pushed. She was pushing well, but this was her first birth and they both knew it might take her a little bit longer than a mother who had given birth before.

Jess looked on anxiously and Adam noticed. 'Put on some gloves and take over coaching Sarah through her breathing for me. I want to use the Doppler to listen in to the baby's heartbeat.'

Jess nodded and grabbed a pair of gloves, smiling nervously at the labouring mother.

When the contraction was over, Sarah grabbed the flannel from Joe, wiping her face and groaning. 'They skip this bit in class. They tell you about dilation, they tell you that you'll push, but they don't tell you how hard, or how long it takes.' She glanced at Jess. 'How long *will* it take?'

'We can't know for sure. Just that every

contraction is one less before they stop. And they will stop. Eventually. You're doing well.' She tried to reassure her as best she could.

Sarah laughed. 'I never thought I'd give birth with a vampire in the room.'

Jess glanced at Adam and he looked back, smiling. What would it have been like to have known Adam as a young boy? As a vampire in a school play! 'Were you Dracula, or something?'

'For my sins. I wasn't very good.'

Sarah laughed. 'Are you kidding me? You made all the girls fall in love with you. Talent *and* devastating good looks? A potent combination!' She sipped her water again. 'Sorry, Joe, but he took my heart for a little while.' She took her husband's hand in hers. 'For about two weeks. And then I fell in love with you.'

'A school romance? That's sweet,' said Jess.

Sarah smiled. 'Well, I don't think Adam was worried about losing my affections. There were plenty of girls to take my place. Oh, God, here comes another!'

Jess looked uncertainly at Adam. The school heart-throb? Yes, she could most definitely see that. How many hearts had he broken in his time?

She could have spent more time feeling resentful that another good-looking man was the same as Eddie, but Sarah had gone into another contraction and Jess stroked her back as she coached her through breathing and pushing once again. On examination, she could feel the top of the baby's head.

'You're doing really well. The baby is right there. Why don't you reach down and feel it?'

She guided Sarah's hands down and the expectant mum gasped.

'Is that the baby? Does it have hair?'

Jess smiled, trying to hold back her tears. Tears for a happiness that would never be hers. 'It certainly does. Do you know what you're having?'

Sarah shook her head. 'We want it to be a surprise.'

'That's brilliant. Do you want us to tell you what it is when it's born? Or do you want to look for yourself?'

'I'd like Joe to tell me.'

'All right.' Jess smiled at Joe. 'When the baby is born we will put him or her on your wife's chest and you can take a look. Does that sound like a plan?'

'It certainly does.'

'Okay, here we go. Big deep breath now—and push!'

Sarah pushed and pushed, a mixture of a growl and a yell escaping her with her effort. It wouldn't be long now. The baby was crowning.

I just need to hold it together for a little while longer. I can do this!

'Okay, stop pushing and just breathe it out for me,' she told Sarah. 'Pant… That's it… Adam, can you get the clamps ready?' She knew the clamps would be needed for tying off the umbilical cord.

They waited for Sarah's next contraction, which came about a minute later. Then Jess guided the baby's head and slowly coached Sarah through pushing and breathing until, at just the right moment, the baby slithered out into the water.

It was a moment of sheer joy and sheer terror.

Jess scooped up the baby from the water, and as it broke the surface it let out a lusty cry. The new mum leant back against the bath, holding her baby against her chest as she began to cry with relief and happiness.

Jess had the briefest of moments to glance

at Adam, to share the happiness and the joy, and then she had to wipe her eyes and remind herself that she was still there to do a job.

'Joe, do you want to see what it is?'

Joe leaned in and lifted up one of the baby's legs. 'It's a boy!'

'Oh, my God, I can't believe it!' Sarah cried more tears of happiness as Jess draped towels around the baby to keep it warm and then applied the clamps to the umbilical cord and got Joe to cut it with a special pair of scissors.

It seemed to Jess that the tension in the room was gone and that suddenly everyone felt just a little bit of bliss. It was a wonderful moment. Filled with joy and rapture. She knew that at some point she would have to check the baby, and she knew that there was still the delivery of the placenta and checking for bleeding, but for now all that could wait. The baby boy was being soothed by his mother and Joe was kissing his wife, tears wetting his cheeks.

Jess was aware that the envy was back. Envy for what this couple had just been through. Becoming a family, going from a twosome to a threesome. Sarah had got pregnant, carried a baby, given birth. And now she would start many years of watching that child grow into an adult.

It was something that she would never get to experience for herself—because she couldn't allow it and she couldn't take the risk. She could never have a child knowing that she might pass on the disease that doomed her. The people in this room had no idea of just how lucky they were.

Adam touched her wrist. 'You okay?'

Her skin burned at his touch and she pulled her hand away, smiling. 'Of course! Why wouldn't I be?'

She bustled about, clearing up supplies and equipment, occupying her hands in the hope that it would stop the tears releasing themselves from her eyes. This was a *happy* moment. This was *their* moment—Joe and Sarah's—and not one she should spoil.

Jess could think of quite a few things she'd like right now. Someone to hold her tight. To wrap their arms around her and make her feel safe. Kiss her. Reassure her. Comfort her. But none of that was meant to be.

I stand alone.

'We won't need most of this equipment now. Why don't you pack it away and get some fresh towels for when we move Sarah to a bed?' Adam suggested. He turned to Sarah. 'Do you want me to give an injection of oxytocin for the placenta?' he asked. 'It will help speed up the expulsion.'

The new mum nodded. 'Yes, please.'

He checked the drug with Jess and prepared the syringe, before injecting the drug into Sarah's thigh. The oxytocin would help the womb contract so that the placenta would come away from the uterine wall.

It didn't seem to take long to work, and soon Adam had placed the placenta in a clinical waste bag, so that it could be disposed of at the hospital when they returned.

Eventually they all helped Sarah get out of the bath and walked her over to the bed, pulling back the sheets and tucking her in. Joe brought a nappy and some clothes for the baby, and Jess carried out the Apgar tests before the baby was dressed. He did well, scoring nine out of ten and only losing a point because of the colouring of his hands and feet, which was normal for a newborn.

'Have you guys decided on a name?' Jess asked.

Sarah looked up at them, pride on her face. 'Owen. Owen Thomas.'

Jess glanced at Joe, and then back at Sarah. 'That's lovely. Absolutely lovely.'

For a moment, Jess watched the new family as they bonded, her heart aching at what had been so cruelly snatched away from her.

'Jess. We need to go,' Adam said softly.

She sniffed and forced a smile. 'Yeah… Congratulations, guys.'

CHAPTER FOUR

ADAM TRIED TO relax on the drive back to the hospital, but it was difficult. Being in a car made him feel antsy, incredibly confined, and as if he was trapped in one small space. He didn't like the claustrophobic feeling that it engendered, so he did his best to ignore it by looking out of the window and trying to take in the beautiful vista that Thorney Island provided.

The mountains in the distance were a beautiful grey-green, with a hint of purple from the heather that littered the countryside. He even noticed a couple of kestrels high in the sky, hovering perfectly as they gazed down at some item of prey beneath them.

He tried to imagine what it must feel like to be as free as a bird. All that space, all that sky, with nothing to contain you. Humans thought they were free, but the truth was that they were trapped. Trapped by rules and regulations, by jobs and homes. Relationships. Family.

Expectations abounded… It wasn't easy and he often wished that he could disappear to some isolated cabin in the middle of nowhere, where there were no people, no expectations, and he could live the life he wanted to. One that was free of fear and apprehension, anxiety and stress.

He knew his parents loved him, but he felt the weight of his mother's expectations. He knew she yearned for him to settle down. To find someone to love. To provide her with grandchildren, even though he'd never told her about what had happened with Anoush. They'd known she was his friend, but that was all.

To watch Sarah and Joe begin their family had given him joy, but it was *for them*. He could be happy for others and watch them take the risk with their hearts, but he'd already had to walk through the grief of losing a loved one he'd planned a future with, and he'd lost Anoush in one of the worst ways possible. No one had been through what he'd been through, and he couldn't expect his mother or anyone else to understand just how he felt.

But he'd noticed something at Sarah and Joe's house.

Jess had been tearful. Uncertain and hesitant at times. And the way she'd looked at Sarah and Joe... As if... As if what?

There had been something going on there and he wasn't sure what. She'd said she wanted to specialise in obstetrics—was that it? Had she just been overcome with happiness at getting to do what she wanted to do? Or had it been something more?

Irritated by his own fear at being in the car, he decided to talk to her about it. He might learn something about her *and* take his mind off his phobia.

'Are you okay?' he asked.

Jess nodded and gave him her default *I'm fine!* smile. 'I'm good.'

'You seemed a little...emotional back there.'

Jess laughed. 'I'm not allowed to get emotional at a birth?'

'Of course you are. But...you're a doctor. You have to have some emotional distance.'

Jess seemed to think for a moment. 'You're

right. I'm probably just hormonal, or something.'

'You sure? I thought it seemed something more than that. You looked…wistful.'

'Wistful?' She laughed, as if it was the most ridiculous thing in the world.

'Almost envious?'

Jess didn't answer straight away. She seemed to be thinking about her response before replying. 'I didn't realise you were watching me so closely.'

He shrugged. 'I'm your mentor. I'm meant to be watching you.' He stared at her a moment longer, his focus more on her than it was on the traffic.

But then there was a strange noise coming from beneath the car and it jolted slightly.

Adam's stomach almost leapt into his mouth.

Jess cursed quietly as she checked her mirrors and indicated that she was pulling over.

'What's going on?' Now he was the one who was uncertain.

'I think we've got a flat.'

She pulled off the road, parking on a grass verge, and turned off the engine. They both got out and looked at the tyres, and found that the back left tyre had indeed been punctured.

'Dammit!'

'Do you have a spare?'

Jess nodded. 'There's one under the boot space.' She popped open the boot and moved the carpet lining to reveal the spare tyre in its compartment. Alongside it sat a small plastic case containing the tools and the jack that would be needed. 'Have you ever changed a tyre before?'

'Nope. But I guess if we can deliver a baby, we can certainly change a tyre together.'

She smiled at him and nodded. 'Okay, let's do it.'

Thankfully, the weather wasn't too bad. The wind was blowing quite strongly, but the sun was out in full force for the start of spring, and it wasn't cold either.

Jess helped jack up the car and Adam began to loosen the nuts on the tyre. Occasionally other cars drove by, but nobody stopped to help except for one farmer in a big blue tractor, who checked to make sure that they were okay. Adam reassured him that they were, and the farmer continued on after wishing them the best of luck.

At last Adam managed to get the old wheel off and Jess wheeled it to one side, laying it down on the grass for a moment before going back to see if Adam needed assistance in lifting the new tyre onto the axle.

'Thanks,' he said.

He had to admit that Jess was easy to work with. She was calm and organised. Most people would get angry or exasperated at getting a flat tyre, but not Jess. She took it all in her stride, and he admired that about her.

She seemed to be a strong, confident woman. Clearly self-sufficient. But he guessed she'd had to be after losing both parents and having no one else. There was a strength of character in her that ran quite deep, and though he found that attractive, he knew he would never do anything about it—no matter how much he wanted to. He wasn't looking for a relationship. He'd had one of those and look what had happened.

He was just fastening the nuts on the new tyre when he heard rifle shots, one after the other, puncturing the air. Something happened within him that caused him to freeze. His breath caught in his throat, his hands stilled, his mouth went dry and his heart began to pound. He stumbled backwards in his urge to hide and take cover, but found that his legs wouldn't move at all.

'Adam?'

He was vaguely aware that Jess was speaking to him, but her voice sounded muffled and far away. His gaze was still fixed on the tyre, but everything around it was beginning to blur and go dark.

'Adam!'

He felt sick, his stomach churning and the trembling worsening, and the rifle shots continued to sound in the air. There were too many, too loud, like an array of fireworks. And even though he tried to tell himself that he was on Thorney Island, not back in Kabul, the logic just did not seem to register in his brain. He was thrown back through time to a desert with hot winds, the smell of cordite and blood, and he began to hyperventilate.

'Anoush...'

He became vaguely aware that someone's hands were on his shoulders and they were trying to get him to look at them, but he couldn't focus on their face. He felt trapped, he felt cornered, and the fear within him was winning.

He tried to scramble further back and fell. He didn't feel the gravel of the road cutting through the palms of his hands. He didn't feel any pain at all. All he felt was fear and terror and the need to flee.

* * *

Anoush. What was Anoush? Was that a word in another language? Or a name?

Jess didn't know what to think. One moment they had been changing her tyre, and she'd been thankful that the focus had moved off her reaction to Sarah and Joe having their baby, and the next Adam had gone as white as a sheet and his eyes had glazed over.

She was aware of rifle shots not far from where they were—was that affecting him? She'd seen this reaction before.

'Adam? Adam! Look at me. *Look...at... me!*'

But she could see by the look in his eyes that he wasn't completely present. That in his mind he was somewhere else completely. She realised the gunshots must have something to do with it. Adam had been in Afghanistan with International Health—she knew that. He seemed traumatised. As if he was suffering from a flashback. Had he been under fire? Had he been attacked?

She knelt in front of him and tried to get him to focus on her face. He was breathing too fast, his eyes flicking from one side to the other as if looking for an escape. She wasn't sure he was seeing the here and now. He was going to pass out if he didn't calm down. He was having a panic attack.

'Adam, it's Jess. You're okay. You're completely safe. I know you can hear gunshots, and I don't know what they're shooting at, but they're miles away. You're safe. Can you hear me? Adam?'

She put her hands either side of his face to make him look at her and somehow her voice must have got through to him, because suddenly he was staring hard at her, still breathing heavily.

'That's it…you're doing brilliantly. Just breathe. Steady your breathing. You're safe. You're okay. I'm looking after you. Nothing will happen to you. Nothing.'

As she held his face in her hands, staring into his eyes from only inches away, she realised just how intimate this was. But she needed to get this right. She needed to calm him down. How beautiful his blue eyes were—even filled with fear. How close they were right now…

Ideally, she would like to take a step back, because she knew how attracted she was to this man and it felt dangerous to be this close. To be helping him in this manner.

She hoped and prayed that she would get

through to him. It was awful to see him like this and she wanted to help. Once he came back to the present, she would step back. Step away. Reluctantly, but she would do it. Because she couldn't get involved with this man. She had nothing to offer him but sadness.

Adam spoke. 'I… I thought that…'

'It's okay. I know what you thought. But you're safe. Okay?'

She stroked his cheek, trying to soothe him with a gentle touch, but suddenly stopped when she realised what she was doing. She pulled her hands away reluctantly, feeling regretful that she had to. But he was getting better. His breathing was more under control. He seemed more present. He was doing well, even though the gunshots were still going on in the distance.

She opened the car door and grabbed a bottle of water and brought it out to him. 'Here—take a drink of this. Just sip it.'

Adam held on to the water bottle, his hands still trembling a little, but he opened it, swallowed some of the water and then tightened the cap and passed it back. 'Thank you. It'll be the clay pigeon shoot at the inn. They do a charity shoot every year. I'd forgotten. I…'

She smiled at him, glad to have been able

to help. She had not expected this. It hadn't even occurred to her that Adam might have returned from his travels a little damaged. He seemed so together. And hadn't he been back for over a year? Had he never addressed this with someone?

She had so many questions, but she didn't want to be the person who asked him before he was ready to talk. Because she very much believed that if someone wanted you to know something about them they would tell you, but only when they were ready to. She did not want to push Adam Campbell. Because if she did, he would drag her further and further into his life, and she was trying to keep him at a distance.

'You sit here for a moment. I'll let down the jack and pack everything away.'

She quickly released the jack and managed to lift the punctured tyre into the boot space. It was a struggle, and a little heavier than she'd expected, but she did it. And when she was done Adam was standing up, waiting for her.

'I'm sorry about that. I didn't mean to…'

Jess brushed away some of the dirt from her top. The black rubber tyre had made a mark on her white blouse. 'It's not a problem. Are you…are you speaking to anyone about this?'

Even now the rifle shots were sounding, and she could tell he still wasn't comfortable. He seemed to flinch at every one.

He didn't answer. He didn't seem to be able to look her in the eye. She wondered if he felt a little embarrassed at revealing a weaker side of himself?

She got into the driver's seat and waited for him to get in on the passenger side. He pulled the door shut and began to put on his seatbelt.

'I'd be obliged if you didn't mention this to anyone,' he said.

'Hey, it's none of my business.'

'I know, but… You helped me out and… I'm sorry you had to see that.'

Jess struggled with what she needed to say. There was so much that was crossing her mind, and it was hard to filter out what was most important.

She looked at him. 'Are you getting help for it?'

'Help? I don't need *help*.' He said the word 'help' as if it was ridiculous.

'I think you have PTSD. I could be wrong—I mean, I'm not a psychologist or anything—but that gunfire really set you off.'

Adam looked down and away. 'I don't have PTSD. It was just…something unexpected, that's all.'

'If you say so.'

She didn't agree—not really. To her, it was obvious. Even though she wasn't trained in mental health. Perhaps if she had been she might have spotted that something was wrong with her father before he took his own life.

'But I don't think this is something you should ignore. You should talk to someone about it. I've seen what happens when people don't share their innermost thoughts and feelings and—'

'Jess, I said I'm fine!' he said. Then he must have realised his tone had been sharper than he'd intended, and he looked at her apologetically. Softened his voice. 'Honestly.'

She stared back, not believing him. 'People have said that to me before.'

Jess started the engine and gave him a look. He at least managed to look a little guilty before he turned away and looked out of the window once again. She indicated and checked her mirrors before pulling out.

There was tension in the air. A little awkwardness. And she really didn't like it.

'I'm sorry. I don't want to push you. I'm sure you know if you need counselling.'

He nodded. 'And I know you're just trying to help. I appreciate that—I do.'

'Well, if you ever want to talk, I hope you'll feel that you can talk to me.'

And she meant it. Even though she wanted to keep him at a distance, her need to make sure another human being was safe overrode any personal desires she had right now. Her father hadn't talked to anyone and he had taken his own life. She'd heard of people coming back from war zones suffering so badly they took their own lives because they couldn't deal with their PTSD, or they turned to drugs or alcohol as a coping mechanism. If she could somehow stop that for Adam, just by offering to lend him an ear, then she would do it.

'Thanks.'

The silence was a little more companionable now, as Jess negotiated them through the traffic that had built up around West Thorney and they headed back towards the hospital.

She wanted to push for more. She wanted to say that he should get help, find someone he could talk to about this, because she really didn't think it was something that was going to go away. Surely he knew that, too?

Adam was medically trained. He must have seen PTSD in others, having worked in war zones abroad. He must know this was something that couldn't just be left to heal on its own. The mind needed looking after just as much as the body did.

Maybe she needed to give him the benefit of the doubt. Give him some time and see how he went. But she knew if she witnessed another event such as this she would insist that he found someone to talk to, because she could not let him carry on untreated. People took their own lives over lesser things.

She parked in one of the doctors' bays and helped Adam carry the equipment back into the hospital. They restocked it before returning it to its designated space, and then disposed of the placenta in the clinical waste.

'Do you want to write up the notes for Sarah?' he asked her.

'Absolutely. Might as well get used to the computer system.'

'Okay. Did Admin set you up with a log-in yet?'

'They said they'd have that done by tomorrow.'

'I'll let you use mine.'

He came around the desk and leant over her to tap in his pass code on the keyboard. She became vitally aware of his closeness and leant back away from him, trying to create some distance.

'What's Anoush?'

Adam stilled. 'What?'

She looked around them to make sure no one was listening. 'Back there, when you… You said "Anoush". What is that?'

He shook his head. 'Nothing you need to worry about.' His fingers flew over the keyboard and she watched each keystroke.

'Chocolate pudding?'

Adam stood up straight as he looked down at her. 'Sorry?'

She smiled. 'Your password is chocolate pudding.'

'You're not meant to look.'

'Yeah, well…sometimes you can't help but see.'

CHAPTER FIVE

ADAM'S MOTHER WELCOMED Jess at the door with a smile that became an unexpected, all-encompassing hug.

At first Jess froze, but then she relaxed into it.

This must be what a mother's love feels like.

Adam was lucky to have both of his parents and not to have experienced loss.

Having never had a mother of her own—not that she could remember anyway—she found Judy's warmth and kindness meant a great deal to her, someone who had been starved of them for so long. And she allowed herself to accept it because surely getting close to Judy wouldn't hurt.

'I'm so pleased you could come tonight.'

'Are you kidding me? I wouldn't have missed it.'

'Good. Come on in! It's getting a bit chilly out there. You too, Adam!'

Jess had decided to walk with him over to his parents' house. She was looking forward to getting to know her boss and his wife better. She might even find out more about Adam, too. Did his parents know of his difficulties? Probably not. Because on the way over Adam had once again sworn her to secrecy about what had happened to him today.

'They don't need to know.'

Considering he was fighting a powerful internal battle, she thought Adam was doing pretty well, presenting himself as an ordinary guy with nothing in his life to worry about. Jess wondered why he hadn't spoken to his parents about what he was going through. But she decided that she wouldn't raise the issue unless he did.

She followed Judy into the house, closing the door behind her. 'Something smells good,' she said.

'I've got some tatties on to go with a stew.'

Jess's stomach rumbled in anticipation. If it tasted half as good as it smelled, then she was in for a treat. And she never made meals like that for herself. Things that took a lot of time to prepare and cook. She was an instant girl. Microwavable meals. Takeout. Something she could grab from the freezer, stick on a baking tray and cook in thirty minutes.

Homely meals made from fresh vegetables that had been peeled and chopped, with meat that had been marinated and stewed, cooked for hours, which would just slide off the bone and melt in her mouth was something she'd never really made. Not since Eddie had left, anyway.

There didn't seem to be much point now she was on her own, and she spent more time at work than anywhere else. Her time off was precious, and she didn't want to stand over a cooker for hours. She didn't have the energy for it.

Maybe I should make the time, if food can smell this good.

'Jess! You're here.'

She instantly turned at the sound of Jack Campbell's voice, a warm smile on her face, and watched as he came out of a room, holding onto a newspaper with one hand and removing his reading glasses with the other.

'Hello, Dr Campbell.'

'Call me Jack.'

She gave him a quick hug.

'How was your first day? Are you overwhelmed with information?'

Jess glanced at Adam. *He'd* overwhelmed her. Very much, and for many different reasons. Looking at him now, she could hardly believe that a few hours ago their faces had been mere inches apart and she'd been staring into his eyes, begging him to come back to her. That kind of thing made them less like strangers.

'A little,' she said.

'Natural. First days are the worst, aren't they?'

'No, it was good. Interesting.'

'Adam showed you everything?'

He showed me more than you'd probably believe.

'Yes, I got the tour.'

'What do you think of the place? Now that you're actually here?'

'It's perfect.'

Jack beamed, clearly proud of what he had built. 'Let me get you a drink. What would you like?'

'Just tea for me.'

'Adam?'

'I'm fine, thanks.'

'How do you take it?' Jack asked.

'White, no sugar,' Adam answered for her, and she smiled at him, thankful for his remembering.

'Why don't you settle yourselves in the living room and I'll call you through when it's ready? It shouldn't be long,' said Judy.

With Judy and Jack gone, she glanced at Adam, who took her jacket and hung it up before leading her into the living room. It was filled with a big squishy sofa, with a ginger cat curled up on one end, and a small fire crackled away in the grate.

'That's Hamish. He's not really a cat. He's a wild animal armed with blades.'

'He looks sweet.'

'He's a con artist. He makes you think he's sweet until you're in range of those claws.'

Jess sat down next to Hamish and the cat opened its eyes and considered her briefly, before standing up, arching his back in a stretch, rubbing up against her, head-bumping her affectionately, and then coiling back into his previous position.

She gave him a stroke. 'He's a big softy.'

'You must have secret powers.'

'Maybe I do!'

Was this flirting? It couldn't be flirting, right? They were just talking, that was all.

It didn't matter that he was smiling at her and looking at her as if she was an amazing person, did it? It didn't matter that every time he smiled at her it made her heart begin thumping away, did it? No, it was just normal conversation. Chit-chat. No subtext. No…flirtation. Just colleagues. Just friends. Nothing in it.

So why did she suddenly feel so nervous? Was it because of the situation? It couldn't be anything else. When you dated a guy, he took you to meet his parents at some point, but she and Adam weren't dating. They'd only just met today!

And, boy, what a long day it had turned out to be. Trying to not have feelings towards Adam, helping him through a panic attack, birthing a baby together… Those kinds of things tended to bring people together.

'What are you two talking about?' Judy asked as she came out of the kitchen, looking at them both as if she'd caught naughty schoolchildren scribbling on the walls.

Jess smiled. 'Hamish has accepted me as one of his own.'

'He purred and everything,' Adam added.

Judy beamed with delight. 'Always trust an animal's reaction to a person, I say. It'll tell you heaps. Jack said he knew you were the right doctor to join us and Hamish has confirmed that. What about you, Adam? What do you think to our Jess?'

Our Jess. She noticed that and felt warmed by the words. It spoke of familiarity and belonging—said that she was *one of them*, part of their family already. And, God damn it, if that didn't almost make her tearful!

But she was curious about what Adam would say, having been put on the spot.

'She's good. Aye.'

Judy laughed. 'Very verbose. Don't go overboard, Adam. Come on, you've worked with her all day! Pay the girl a compliment!'

She saw Adam give his mother a stare, as if she was making him do something he didn't want to do, and she almost laughed. It was funny to see him looking so awkward. She didn't *need* him to give her a compliment. She didn't *need* him to say that she was wonderful, or whatever, but it still would be nice.

Adam turned to look at her, a rueful smile on his face. 'She's very kind. Caring. Empathetic.' He turned back to his mother. 'Enough for you?'

'I don't know. Is it enough for *you*, Jess?'

Jess laughed, feeling happier than she had

in ages. 'Absolutely. More than enough.' And without thinking she turned back to Adam and gave him a wink.

He tried to suppress a smile, and she liked it that she seemed to be having a secret conversation with him.

Judy checked her watch. 'Right. Dinnertime! Who wants to help me lay the table?'

Jess raised a hand, loving every second of being with Adam and his family. Who knew it could be like this? Family that stuck together and loved one another. That camaraderie, the in jokes, the gentle ribbing of each other.

She'd experienced none of that with her own father. He'd been a distant man in many ways, never one to be over-generous with hugs or praise, and he'd told her once that he was teaching her to be independent and to stand on her own two feet.

How long had he known about his Huntington's? How long had he kept it a secret from her? Had he been preparing her for the day he would leave her? Had he taken his own life thinking that she was settled with Eddie and she wouldn't be alone to get through her grief? Had he thought that Eddie would stay and support her after she'd read his suicide note telling her why he'd done what he had?

He'd been wrong. Eddie had left her, unable to cope with the news that his girlfriend would slowly deteriorate and die sooner rather than later. With the news that their hope to have a family had been destroyed, because Jess would never have a child knowing that she could pass on the disease.

He'd just walked away! Left her a note, just like her father. As if only his grief counted. Had Eddie not realised just how much *she'd* been grieving, too? For the loss of the family she'd been dreaming of. The loss of the future she'd imagined. The loss of her own father and the father of her future children?

I lost this—what I'm seeing today. Lost what it's like to be a family.

She helped get out plates and cutlery with Adam and kept stealing glances at him, her heart warming with every one—especially if he caught her doing it and smiled back. And although she tried to tell herself to stop doing it, that maybe it could be misconstrued, the yearning to be a part of his family, his loving circle, was strong.

I can have it for one night, surely?

What harm would it cause? She was just

smiling at him. Appreciating his good looks. The welcome she felt here. It wasn't as if they were on a date. She'd been invited to dinner by her boss and his wife, Adam hadn't asked her to come.

She suspected Judy had hopes that Jess might have feelings for her son. She could see it in her eyes, her smile, and the blatant way she sat Jess directly opposite Adam.

Her stomach rumbled in anticipation as Judy brought the food over in steaming dishes.

'This looks amazing,' Jess said.

'It's just an old stew recipe that my mother used to make.'

'Well, if it's half as delicious as it smells, then I may just want to eat the whole thing myself.'

Judy smiled her thanks at the compliment. 'I heard you two had an exciting day?'

Jess looked at Adam. Had he said something after all? Which bit was she talking about? 'Oh?'

'I heard you two went to Sarah's house and delivered her baby?'

So Adam hadn't mentioned his panic attack. She wasn't surprised at that and, even though this was a family of medical professionals, and Judy obviously knew who Sarah was, she didn't want to share too much. 'Yes, we did.'

'I guess that's a good way to spend your first day at work.'

Adam nodded. 'It was nice to have a happy result.'

'That's all any of us ever want.'

Jess thought about any happy results she'd had in her life and, apart from passing her exams to become a doctor, she couldn't think of anything that had truly made her happy. She'd never really had a mum, her father had taken his own life, she'd been diagnosed with a life-limiting disease, her one relationship hadn't worked out... It wasn't much to cheer about. She was just plodding on, day after day, trying to make the world believe that she was happy and successful and enjoying life, when in reality she was full of doubt and fear.

But she would have liked to know what it felt like to come home to someone she could speak to. Someone who would respond to her with love and kindness, who would envelop her in the kinds of hugs that Judy gave and understand and comfort her, make her feel human again.

Because sometimes—not that she'd told

anybody—she felt as if she was a robot. Going through the motions. Just getting through the day, waiting for a malfunction to occur. It would happen one day, and she had the genetic results to prove it.

'I heard it was a little boy.'

Jess had just put a forkful of lamb into her mouth, so she simply smiled at Judy and nodded.

'I know her mother. No doubt I'll see her tomorrow and she'll have loads of pictures to show me. Maybe one day I'll be able to do the same in return. Adam has yet to provide me with any grandchildren!'

'Mother!' Adam growled.

Judy laughed. 'I'm not telling you something you don't already know! What about you, Jess? Do you ever see yourself having children?'

She put down her knife and fork and grabbed her napkin to dab at her mouth and think. Children were totally out of the question for her. She knew there was the possibility of genetic testing if she ever changed her mind and went down that route, but that wasn't the point. Why would she have a child, even if it was healthy and not live to see that child grow up? Have that child lose its mother? She couldn't put a child through that.

But that was too complicated to share with them all. They didn't need to know her problems. 'I'm so busy with work right now I've not really thought about it,' she said, trying to say it nonchalantly.

'Well, I've lived with doctors my entire life, so I know you'll have to think about it soon. Whether to have a child before you specialise or after. If you choose after, you'll probably be in your late thirties, early forties, and time will be ticking! But if you have a family before you specialise you'll have to consider childcare and how much of your child's life you're happy to miss. No matter what you do, your patients will always come first—it's a hard life, being the child of a doctor.'

'I think the decision as to what Jess does with her life is hers to make,' Adam said, sounding irritated.

'I know that, dear. I was just mentioning it.'

All this talk about children and having babies was really getting to Jess. She could hardly swallow her food now, the lump in her throat felt so big. 'Could I use your bathroom?' she managed.

'It's up the stairs, first door on the left,' Adam said.

'Thank you.'

She excused herself and hurried up the stairs as her tears began to fall. Behind her, she heard Adam admonishing his mum about getting too personal.

She ran into the bathroom and closed the door behind her, sinking to the floor and allowing her tears to fall.

How much of your child's life you're happy to miss...

She would miss all of it, because she wouldn't have one.

Jess had thought she'd run out of tears about this. About never having a baby. The grief for something she hadn't even had. The loss of a dream. A future. A baby to hold in her arms.

It was all too much to bear.

CHAPTER SIX

THE NEXT DAY, Jess discovered that she would be working with Adam in the Well Woman Clinic. They had a full morning of appointments—changing or fitting coils, performing cervical smears, inserting implants.

She felt incredibly awkward after last night. She'd emerged from the bathroom after splashing her face with water and giving herself a stern talking-to in the mirror.

You will not dwell on this! You will not! Now, go down those stairs and show them how wonderful a person Jess is!

She was very good at putting on a mask. She'd had years of preparation. Pretending at school that it didn't matter to her that everyone else had a mother and she didn't. Pretending that it didn't matter that her father never gave her hugs or congratulations when she got high marks in class or exams, that his occasional recriminations that she could have done better didn't hurt. Pretending that she was coping at his funeral. Pretending that she was fine about finding out she carried the Huntington's gene. Pretending that she was okay when Eddie left her.

She absolutely refused to show the world that she was hurting, because who the hell cared? No one in her life, anyway, and wallowing in misery led nowhere.

Jess had a goal. A goal to be a great doctor. And she held that goal in front of her at all times, like a carrot on a stick.

She'd been able to tell when she came down from the bathroom that Adam had said something to his parents, because the atmosphere had changed. The conversation had remained light and well away from anything that might be considered personal.

About an hour after they'd finished eating, Jess had felt so uncomfortable that she had been the one who had changed the happy dynamic of the family that she'd pleaded extraordinary tiredness and said that she would be going home.

Adam had profusely apologised.

'It's fine!' she'd said.

'No, it's not! She had no right to ask you those questions!'

'Adam, honestly, forget about it. I'm not upset.'

But she had been. Upset and guilty.

What would Jack and Judy think of her now? What did *Adam* think? He was the one who mattered. He was the one she would be working closely with.

She needed him to see her as a highly competent professional.

She wanted him to like her.

She wanted him to wrap his arms around her and—

Whoa, there. Hang on a second...

That wasn't ever going to happen. She needed to stop thinking of Adam in such a way. Forget he was too attractive for his own damned good.

I am off the market!

She was faulty goods. She should never even have been on the stall in the first place!

I have to remember that the only thing I have to offer Adam is heartbreak and grief.

Adam had spent a restless night. His mind had tormented him with the look in Jess's eyes last night at the dinner table. His mother had asked that indelicate question and although most people would probably have just laughed it off, or given an actual answer, he'd seen the torment and upset in that look.

She'd tried to hide it. He'd seen her internal battle with herself. But he could have sworn that when she'd stood to leave the table her eyes had been glistening with tears.

Well… He wasn't ashamed to say he'd had quite a conversation with his mother before Jess had made it back downstairs.

Adam knew something about grief. He'd been through it and he could see it in others. Jess had lost her father, was all alone in the world, and probably dreaming of the day she would settle down and have children—finally have a family to call her own. His mother, hassling Jess to choose a time to listen to her her biological clock, had been most rude!

And now they had to work together. He wanted her to feel comfortable with him. Not to feel embarrassed about last night. Not to feel as if she had to explain. Because she didn't have to explain anything.

He liked her. Very much. Probably more than he ought to. And, even though he'd told himself many times over the past year that he would not get involved romantically with anyone ever again, he'd tossed and turned last night, trying to fight off images of what it would have been like to wrap his arms around her and hold her close. To protect her. To care for her. What it might be like to spend time with her and learn more about her...to make her laugh.

Her voice, her eyes, her compassion and her kindness all drew him in, despite his logical thoughts to the contrary and his brain screaming at him that getting close to another woman would only bring heartbreak.

It was confusing, but he kept telling himself that he was okay. That it was fine to be with her because he was just instructing her in the ways of the hospital. She was here to learn and would soon be standing on her own two feet anyway.

They set up the clinic so that Adam would sit and do the admin on the computer, speaking to the patients and explaining what was about to be done, checking their preferences for contraception, while Jess would perform smears and coil fittings, with Adam assisting if necessary.

Their first patient was a young woman who had a six-month-old baby. Vicky Collins came into the room, pushing a pram. She was here to have a contraceptive implant for the first time, and once she'd sat down in the chair and got settled Adam began asking her some questions to establish her state of health and previous contraception methods, and how the implant might differ.

'So, can you tell me which arm is your dominant one?'

'I'm right-handed.'

'Okay, so we'll insert the implant in your left arm, on the inner side of the arm just below the skin. What day of your cycle are you on?'

'Day two.'

'That's perfect. So, once it's in, you shouldn't have to use any other type of contraception. I'm assuming that because you have your period right now you're not pregnant?'

Vicky laughed. 'Definitely not.'

'And you understand the benefits and the risks?'

'I do.'

'I'll give you a leaflet to take home anyway—in case you have any queries—but you can always contact us if you're unsure of anything. Do you have any questions now?'

Vicky shook her head.

'Okay, then, we'll get on with it. If you'd

like to lie on the examination table, we'll get everything set up.'

Jess had already prepared the equipment trolley. There was a sterile surgical drape, some gloves, antiseptic solution, a syringe prefilled with local anaesthetic, a piece of sterile gauze, an adhesive bandage and a pressure bandage. He would do this first procedure, as Jess hadn't yet been signed off on competency for contraceptive implants.

With Vicky lying on her back, Adam flexed her non-dominant arm and elbow and gave it an external rotation, so that her wrist was level with her ear. He identified the insertion site, which was three or four inches above the medial epicondyle of the humerus bone, and then felt for the groove between the biceps and the triceps muscles, knowing that he needed to avoid going too deep there, as that was where large blood vessels and nerves lay. He needed to insert the implant just underneath the skin.

Using a sterile marker, he made two marks on the arm—one where the implant would be inserted and the second mark a few centimetres proximal to the first. The second mark would serve as a direction guide during insertion. He cleaned the insertion site with the antiseptic solution and then anaesthetised the area before Jess handed him the disposable implant applicator from its blister pack.

He removed the protective cover from the needle and with his free hand stretched the skin around the insertion site, puncturing the skin with the tip of the needle, sliding it in to its full length. Then he unlocked the slider on the applicator by pushing it down until it stopped, knowing that the implant was then in position. He removed the applicator and verified the presence of the implant in Vicky's arm by palpating the area.

Jess applied a small adhesive bandage over the insertion site after getting Vicky to feel where the implant was, so that she would recognise how it felt.

'Wow, that feels weird.'

'You'll get used to it.' Adam smiled and then applied a pressure bandage with sterile gauze, to minimise any bruising she might experience. 'You can remove this bandage in about a day, but leave the small bandage on for three to five days, okay?'

'That's fine. Are we all done?'

'Absolutely. And the baby slept throughout.'

'He's a good sleeper.'

Adam gave her the information leaflet whilst Jess cleared up the equipment and wiped down the equipment trolley ready for the next procedure. They waved Vicky good-bye, and when she'd left the room Adam supplied the details of the procedure completed to her patient record.

'That went well,' he said.

'It did. It's nice when everything goes smoothly.'

'Unlike last night,' he said.

'I've told you—you don't need to apolo-gise. Your mum's of a different generation—she's used to asking people questions like that.'

'Well, she won't do it again.'

'Honestly, it was fine.'

He knew he wouldn't get her to admit that it hadn't been.

'Fair enough. Next patient is here for a coil removal and replacement. You want to get set up for that and I'll call her in?'

Jess turned to open a cupboard and get out the equipment they would need. Adam watched her work for a moment. She seemed to be an intensely private person, almost in-troverted, quite content to hide away from life on this little backwater island that was his own sanctuary.

Why had she come here when she could have gone anywhere else and for probably much more pay? Was it simply because this place was where she'd once found happiness with her father? Because being here made her feel closer to him? How alone did she feel?

He was glad that she was here. She'd helped him yesterday through a very difficult moment. He'd not had an attack like that before, and had always downplayed what had happened in Afghanistan and the reasons why he'd decided to finally come home.

Initially, he'd been mortified at the idea of Jess having seen him freak out, but then he'd been very grateful that it had been her and no one else. She'd told him to seek help, and he appreciated her caring about him. That was why he would do the same thing for her. Look out for her. Protect her. Return the favour and keep her secrets.

He opened his mouth to say something, but there was a knock at their door. Their next patient. He bit his lip and called her through.

Later on, Adam found Jess in the hospital cafeteria. It wasn't a big place, but big enough for someone to grab coffee, maybe a slice of cake, or even a hot meal between twelve and two. She was at one of the window tables, with what looked like a cappuccino and a Danish pastry in front of her, and the sunlight shone in her hair. She was reading something on her phone, with a little frown line between her eyebrows to show that she was concentrating.

'Mind if I sit?' He gestured at the chair opposite.

Her face lit up and she put down her phone. 'Please do.'

'Quite a busy morning, wasn't it?'

'I like being kept busy.' She smiled at him.

With a sharp pang in his gut, he once again realised just how beautiful she was, and just how attracted to her he was.

He'd already noticed that, of course—after all, he was a man. The second he'd seen her he'd noticed. He'd just sucked in a deep breath at that moment in time, and told himself that it didn't matter what she looked like because she was here to do a job. There was no way in hell he was going to act on any attraction he felt. Not after what had happened to Anoush.

He looked at her across the table and smiled, feeling his heart and his stomach going all manner of crazy. He couldn't help it. He wanted to fight the feeling and embrace it, ignore it and explore it. His head was a mess! How was she managing to do this to him?

Anoush had been the love of his life and he'd never thought he could be attracted to anyone ever again—and yet here he was. Trying to fight it.

Was it because Jess knew something about him that no one else did? Had that secret united them?

He didn't know.

All he did know was that something inside him kept on telling him he needed to get to know this beautiful woman more.

CHAPTER SEVEN

'Is JESS OKAY?' asked his dad.

Adam nodded. 'She's fine.'

'Not upset about the other night?'

Adam shrugged.

After Anoush, Adam had told himself that he would never get close to another person again. That he would never feel as strongly for anyone as he had for Anoush. That he would never again feel that rush of feeling in his heart.

And yet something was happening between him and Jess. Something intimate that he didn't yet understand. And because he was feeling sensitive about that, when his father had asked about Jess he'd felt a wave of protection come over him. But he didn't want to upset his parents any more than they already were. He knew they still felt bad about the other night at dinner.

'I guess the two of you are okay working together?' asked his father.

'We are.' Adam wanted to be able to say that they were more than okay. That they were actually working very well together indeed. That he thought she was a very fine addition to their medical team. But he knew if he said anything like that his parents might read more into it than he wanted them to.

He knew how keen they were for him to settle down and meet someone. They'd never known about his romantic involvement with Anoush. He'd kept that back from his stories of being abroad. He'd been going to tell them when he had something to tell, and the day he'd asked Anoush to marry him had been the happiest of his life when she'd said *yes*. He'd planned to video call his parents that night and tell them about the wonderful woman he was going to marry, but he'd never got that chance, because that was the day they'd been ambushed and he'd lost her in a hail of bullets.

Why tell them about his lost fiancée now? Why give them that happiness and then the pain of snatching it away from them? It would be cruel. Bad enough that he had to bear it— but them, too…?

'That's good. I'm glad. After all, you're going to be seeing a lot of each other.'

Adam raised an eyebrow.

'Well, you two are working together and you're living in the same building. I'm assuming she'll give you lifts to and from work?'

Adam relaxed. 'I guess she will.'

But he told himself that if he was going to be spending all this time with Jess then he needed to instil some rules into himself. No more looking into her eyes and imagining how it might feel to touch her face. No telling her that she was beautiful. No more being aware of how, when she blushed, the colour slowly rose into her cheeks and made her eyes glisten. No more letting his heartbeat accelerate when she was near. No more.

He would be strictly professional. Work only. Colleagues. Friends. He'd allowed a shared secret to draw them close, but he knew what happened when he thought everything was going brilliantly. The world had a way of playing with him.

He trusted her to keep his secret. He was depending upon her to do that. And in return he would give her the respect and distance they both deserved.

Jess had come to this island to find happi-

ness and her own little sanctuary, the same
way he had when he'd returned home. He
would make sure that she got that—because
she deserved that small measure of peace exactly the way he did.

The next day Jess was working with Adam
in their minor surgery clinic.

These cases weren't anything overly exciting—treating ingrown toenails, excising
cysts, removing lumps—but it was a clinic
that Adam enjoyed. He could be hands-on,
and it gave him a chance to sit and talk to
his patients about things other than their ill-
health. Most of them wanted to chat, to pass
the time of day. It was always pleasant, and
at the end of it he usually left work knowing
that he had made a difference in someone's
life that day.

And that was what it was all about. Making
a difference. Making somebody feel better.
Making someone smile inside. Because ever
since he'd lost Anoush he'd come to realise
that it wasn't always about the smiles on the
outside—the smiles that you could see.

Those smiles were often a mask, hiding
someone's true feelings. It was inner happiness that mattered more than anything else.

He'd found a new way of life for himself back here on Thorney, even though he was here alone, and he'd come to accept that Anoush would never see the place he called home, where they'd planned to settle down. He'd never be able to bring her back to meet his parents. He was here alone and he accepted that fact. Welcomed it. Used it as a wall.

Everyone had walls. Some were smaller than others, but that didn't mean they weren't as important. Each wall had been built from a pain.

And it might not be considered much, removing a cyst, or a lipoma, or an ingrowing toenail, but if it took away someone's discomfort, took away some of their pain, then that had to be a good thing. And he might be the only person that patient spoke to all day.

'So, who have we got next?' asked Jess.

Adam was at the computer, looking at the appointment list. They had eight patients today in this clinic, and so far he had dealt with a cyst on someone's hand and a chalazion on an eyelid—a blocked oil gland.

'Bruce Moorefield. Aged seventy-two. Lipoma on his back. I think I'll let you do this one.'

Jess lit up at the prospect, and he tried not to feel good because he'd made her feel that way. He simply smiled and nodded and tried to force his feelings back inside the box where they belonged. But all he could think about was that he'd made her happy by suggesting she do a procedure.

Such a simple thing, but it mattered. She'd said she liked to keep busy, so he'd given her the more complex procedure to do because he'd known she would like it.

He liked making her happy.

'He came in to see me a couple of weeks ago,' he told her. 'He'd been wearing a back brace and the lipoma was beginning to become irritated, so I said we would remove it. It's just under the skin, soft and doughy to the touch, and it moves easily with light pressure. About three inches in diameter.'

'Okay. Shall I call him in?'

'Yep. Go ahead.'

He watched her walk to the door, all bright and breezy, and call Bruce in. Jess looked very pretty today, in a blue blouse and dark trousers. She'd swept her hair into a messy up-do and the odd tendril hung down here and there. He wondered what it would be like to take those glasses off her and pull her hair free and watch it swish down…

Stop. It.

He cleared his throat and she looked at him.

'Okay?' she asked.

'Just a wee frog.'

A smile from her—and it was like being punched in the gut. What was wrong with him?

Bruce Moorefield ambled into the room. They both welcomed him in, and Adam bade him sit down, just to go over the basics before the procedure began.

'I know you said it wasn't anything to worry about, Doc, but my daughters are worried that it might be dangerous.'

'They don't need to worry. Lipomas are usually benign. They're just masses of fat cells that have lumped together. We always take a biopsy, just in case, and send it for pathology, but it is extremely rare for one of them to become cancerous.'

'I trust you completely,' said Bruce. 'It's just…you know what family can be like.'

Adam nodded and smiled.

'So, how do we do this?' Bruce asked.

'We mark out where we want to make the

incision—it's usually just a small cut in the skin—and then the lipoma can be squeezed out. It's all done under local anaesthetic, so you shouldn't feel a thing. And, like I said, we'll send it off to be checked under the microscope, but that's common procedure.'

'Great. Let's do it.'

Jess smiled. 'Okay, let's get you up on this bed. If you can remove your shirt and lie on your front for me?'

'No problem. But it's a long time since I stripped off in front of a pretty young lady.'

'I'll turn my back.'

Jess smiled and pretended to straighten her equipment. Then she removed the cover from her sterile field and put on her apron and gloves.

Adam was on the opposite side of the bed, placing a drape over the cyst. It had a pre-cut aperture in it, so that Jess could see the lipoma. He used a sterile marker to make a dotted line around the outside edge of the cyst, and then drew a line down the middle, where the incision would be.

'Okay with that?' he asked Jess.

'Yes. That's perfect. Thank you. Okay, Bruce. I'm going to give you some local anaesthetic, but I'm going to need to insert it all around the lipoma. This is the uncomfortable bit and you might feel a little sting here and there. Are you ready for me to go ahead?'

'I'm good. You do what you have to do, Doc,' Bruce said, from his position face-down on the table.

'Okay. But if you need me to stop at any point, then you tell me.'

Adam watched as Jess drew up the anaesthesia into the syringe and used the lines that Adam had drawn previously as markers. She began injecting the numbing agent. It only took a moment or two.

'So, Bruce,' said Adam. 'The last time we met you told me your daughter was waiting to adopt. How's that going? Has she heard anything?'

'Well, yes, she did hear something. There's the chance that they might be getting a new wee one, but there's so much red tape, we don't know for sure.'

'I think adoption is amazing!' said Jess. 'You get to choose your family.'

'Aye, you do.'

Jess used a pair of tweezers to pinch at various points of Bruce is back. 'Can you feel me touching you?'

'Not a thing.'

'Good. So, I'm going to make a start. If you feel anything—any pain, anything unpleasant—you tell me and I'll stop and give you more anaesthetic, okay?'

'Will do.'

Jess picked up a scalpel and began her initial incision down the line that Adam had drawn. As she worked, Adam used gauze to wipe away the blood that began to build so that she had a clear field to work in. Occasionally he had to use a cautery to stop some of the more determined bleeds.

They worked well together. He didn't get in her way and she didn't get in his. They were like a well-oiled machine. Almost as if they'd worked together for years, rather than days.

'I think I need to make this incision just a little bit bigger,' she muttered, having given the lipoma a squeeze.

'I agree,' said Adam.

She used her fingers to feel inside the incision and made sure the lipoma was not attached to any of the surrounding structures beneath the skin, and then she began to squeeze the lipoma out. It was quite stubborn to begin with, but eventually, with a bit of manipulation, it began to be exposed.

Jess had started to grab hold of it and fully

remove it when her arm suddenly spasmed and her hand contracted.

Bruce flinched. 'Ooh, I felt that!'

Jess stood there in shock, looking down at her arm and hand.

'Is everything all right?' asked Adam.

He'd seen the spasm—the way her whole arm had moved as if of its own accord.

'I...' Jess looked shell-shocked.

Adam frowned, seeing apprehension and fear in Jess's face, watching her cheeks not colouring, but paling. But they had a patient on the table, and he must come first. He would speak to Jess about this later. It had just been a spasm, surely? Everyone had them.

He stepped forward and took the implements from her hands. 'I'll finish up. Why don't you go make a cup of tea? Bruce won't mind—will you, Bruce?'

'No, I don't mind which of you does it. Is it out?'

'Just about,' said Adam.

He nodded his head towards the door, indicating that Jess should go, as suggested. Jess ripped off her gloves and apron, slamming them into the clinical waste bin and hurrying from the room.

He'd never seen her look so terrified. Although it was almost akin to the way she'd looked when his mother had started asking her questions about having children...

He'd never concentrated so hard on a patient, even though all he wanted to do was run after Jess and see if she was all right.

CHAPTER EIGHT

JESS HADN'T THOUGHT it would happen so quickly.

Well, now it had.

She hurried down the corridor, not sure what she was doing or where she was going. Should she tell Jack? Judy? No one?

She needed someone to tell her that it was probably just a spasm, nothing more. But not Adam. Oh, no, not Adam.

Of all of them she wanted him to see her the way she aspired to be—brilliant, able, trusted, strong. One of the team. She couldn't bear the idea of him finding out about this. He was becoming a good friend as well as a colleague, and she really, really liked him. As long as he didn't know about it she could maintain the illusion she'd fought so hard to create—that everything was right in her world. That she was okay.

She didn't need him worrying about her—not when he had his own problems to deal with. Adam was vulnerable, and he cared, and if he found out about this it would change who they were to each other.

Jack wasn't in his office. She asked around but nobody seemed to have seen him. Out of breath, she stopped for a moment and looked down at her hand. It felt weird. As if it didn't belong to her. But was she imagining that because she was fearing the worst? She massaged it, turning it this way and that. It twitched again, and this time she felt the movement in her entire arm, felt both her hands trembling.

Using her good left hand, she held her arm against her body and pressed it tight. What was going on? There was a free computer at the nurses' station and, unable to think of anything else to reassure herself, she sat down at the desk, typed in her newly created password and looked up the word that she'd hoped not to look for for a long time yet.

Chorea.

Chorea. An abnormal involuntary movement disorder. A dyskinesia. Characterised by brief, irregular movements. A hyperkinetic movement disorder. Commonly seen in Huntington's disease, a neurodegenerative disorder.

She'd seen this symptom before, in her father. At the time he'd dismissed it and said it was nothing, and she'd believed him. Why wouldn't she? He was her father and she'd always listened to him, believed him when he said he had some sort of intermittent tremor. But it hadn't been that, and now she knew he'd begun to hide his symptoms, seeing her less and less—until that final dinner when she'd insisted he come to hers and Eddie's so she could make the announcement that they were trying to start a family.

It hadn't ever been a hard choice as to what to do with her life. She'd always thought of becoming a doctor, and the proudest day of her life had been walking across that platform to collect her medical degree. She'd just imagined she'd have a lot longer to practice.

Now she was beginning to understand her father's fear.

She'd been angry with him after she'd read his suicide note. He should have told her! He hadn't needed to keep it a secret! She was a doctor!

In his note, he'd written that taking his own life had been the only thing to do, so that she wouldn't have to care for him as his condition got worse. He'd thought that he was relieving her of a burden. But perhaps he hadn't thought about what effect it would have on her—him leaving her all alone in the world.

He'd left her the house and all his worldly goods, the savings he had in the bank. And she'd thought she'd get through it because she'd had Eddie at her side.

At least until her blood results had come through.

She'd thought hearing the diagnosis was her most terrifying moment in life, but it wasn't. This was.

'Jess?'

She looked towards the voice, saw Adam strolling down the corridor towards her, and instantly used the mouse to close down the screen on the computer, so that he didn't see what she had been looking at.

'Hey.'

'Are you all right? What happened back there?'

'Nothing. I just had a weird spasm, that's all…' She hated lying to him.

Adam frowned, looking as if he didn't

quite believe her. 'It happens to the best of us. We're human. But when it happened to you... You looked horrified. Terrified. Like something else was happening.'

She stood up, pushing her chair neatly behind the desk, smiling as brightly as she possibly could. 'Honestly, it was nothing. Look—I'm fine.'

She held both hands out in front of her, so that he could see that they were once again steady, praying inwardly that her body wouldn't choose this exact moment to go into spasm again.

She got away with it. Her arms and hands remained steady.

But Adam looked at her with question and stepped forward, taking her right hand and arm in his, flexing and straightening the arm, turning her wrist this way and that, palpating her shoulder joint, checking everything.

She tried her hardest not to blush, not to allow heat to suffuse her cheeks at his touch, but it was difficult. She'd spent a lot of time thinking about what it might be like to be close to this man, wanting him to touch her, and now that he was—even though it was in a medical way, and not an erotic one—she couldn't stop her body responding.

She thanked heaven that his fingers were not on her pulse-points measuring her heart-rate!

'You see? I'm fine.' She pulled her hand free and folded her arms, lifting her chin as if in challenge.

'You would tell me if there was something bothering you?' he asked.

'Of course,' she replied, in a lie that came too easily—much to her disgust.

She'd never thought about this moment. Never thought that she would have to lie to him. Keep secrets. She'd hated the fact that her father had done it and now she was doing the same thing!

But I'm trying to protect him.

The way her father had tried to protect her. How easy that kind of behaviour was to slip into. She began to realise just how her father had felt. Lying to protect the person he'd loved.

But had his lies protected her? All those times he'd told her he was fine…all those times he'd told her he was okay. Had she believed him? Yes—naïvely, she had. Because he had been her father and he had loved her, and he'd been all she'd had. Of course she'd believed him. She had trusted him to tell her the truth, because what was love without trust?

She looked up at Adam, fighting the tears that were threatening to spill from her eyes. She could see in his face that he didn't quite believe her and that *hurt*. She didn't want to hurt him, she didn't want to lie to him, but she couldn't think of anything else to do. And she so much wanted to tell him everything, but she couldn't just blurt it out. It wouldn't be right. There was a time and a place for this kind of thing, and this wasn't it.

He stared back—hard. 'I'll find out, you know. If something is wrong… If it's escaped your attention… That's what doctors do—find out what's wrong.'

'I know. But you don't have to look after me, Adam. I'm perfectly fine.'

He shook his head. 'You're not. And you should let me help you.'

It took every ounce of strength she had, not to just tell him everything there and then. The urge to unburden herself was incredibly strong, but she fought it to the bitter end, no matter how hard it was to concentrate when he was holding her hand in such a way.

He frowned and she let out a breath, sinking against the desktop as if she'd just fought an incredible battle. Had she won or lost? She didn't know. But what she did know was that she was exhausted. Fear was exhausting.

She wondered how long she would be able to maintain her lie. He would see through it. Instinctively, she felt that he would somehow know.

'Why should I let you help me? Because you're a doctor? I'm fine, Adam. Please just leave me alone.'

And she walked away, biting her bottom lip to stop herself from crying.

Adam lay in bed, staring at the ceiling. He'd not been able to settle all night and now he lay flat on his back, staring upwards, wondering about the woman in the apartment above who seemed to have every moment of his focus.

Jess.

She was keeping something from him, but he didn't know what. He'd watched her during the procedure earlier on and she'd been happy, smiling, confident—sure of everything she was doing, chatting to the patient, keeping him at ease, and then…

Something.

Something had happened to her arm—a

spasm. Brief, no more than a millisecond in length. It happened to doctors around the world every day—after all they were only human, and human bodies twitched on occasion—but Jess had looked down at her hands in such horror, in such disbelief, her cheeks paling.

He hadn't understood what was happening but had known he must quickly reassure their patient. And as Jess had fled the room Adam had looked down at the open incision, trying his hardest to concentrate on what was most important, finding it difficult to do so. All his mind had wanted to settle on was why that spasm had terrified Jess so much. Why she had reacted so strongly to it? They had to be something he didn't know about.

Adam tried to think. Was the spasm part of something bigger? And, if so, what? Muscle spasms could be caused by all sorts of things and all sorts of conditions, from the benign to something more serious. Was it right that her reaction should make him think that something more serious was most definitely going on? Or was he just seeing the worst, because that was what he was used to seeing?

Jess was becoming a friend—a good friend—even though he'd only known her for such a short period of time, and he was used to looking out for his friends. Protecting them, keeping them safe from harm... He'd not been able to keep Anoush safe, but he was damn well sure he would do his best to look out for Jess.

And... I don't know...she's special to me. No matter how much I try for her not to be.

His eyes began to grow heavy and he allowed them to close, looking for the sanctuary of sleep, where worries and concerns had no place.

Screaming the like of which she had never heard before in her entire life woke Jess from her sleep. She jolted awake, heart pounding, semi-upright in bed, looking around her for the source.

Who the hell was screaming?

She quickly realised that it was coming from the flat below her.

Adam's flat.

She threw off her bed covers and grabbed her robe, hurrying to the front door. She quickly unlocked it and hurried down the stairs to the next floor, began banging on Adam's front door.

'Adam! *Adam!*'

The screaming stopped but she kept hammering her fist on the door until it was finally opened by a half-naked, sweating Adam.

He wore pyjama bottoms and was barefoot and bare-chested, his eyes dull and his hair mussed around his head. At any other time she would have appreciated the sight. He was very well built, his muscles defined without being overly so, with a smattering of chest hair. But she shoved to one side her desire to examine him more carefully. He looked so far away, distant, as if he was seeing another place.

She made him make eye contact with her as she had done once before, placing her hands on either side of his face, knowing this would help bring him back to the present.

'What's going on? Are you okay? I heard screaming.'

He gently pulled her hands away, clearly back in reality and obviously not happy to find himself rescued by Jess once again.

'I'm fine. It was just a dream. A bad dream.'

'It sounded like more than that. It sounded like you were being tortured.' She'd never heard a sound like it before and she hoped never to hear it again.

He smiled and wiped the sweat from his brow with his forearm. 'I'm sorry I woke you.'

'I'm sorry you think you have to go through whatever this is alone,' she returned.

He looked away from her, down towards the floor, before looking back up, his eyes challenging. 'I could say the same to you. Something is bothering you, but you won't tell me what it is. You know, you *could* share.'

She stared back. 'So could you.'

They looked at each other in a stalemate for a long time, until finally Adam backed away. 'I guess you'd better come in.'

She stepped in, pulling her robe tight around her like a shield, and followed him through to his living room.

Adam switched on the light and headed to the kitchen to make them both a drink. 'Tea? Coffee?'

'I'm not sure that's wise if you want to get back to sleep.'

'Don't worry, it's decaf.'

She smiled. 'Nothing for me, thanks.'

He switched off the kettle and leant back against the counter. 'So, are you going to tell me what happened today?'

No. She wouldn't let him make this about

her. 'You were the one screaming. Are you going to tell me what's happening with you?'

He sighed. 'I guess I'm not going to win this one, am I?'

'You're not going to get better unless you have some counselling. Adam, I think you've got PTSD—and that's not something that just goes away all by itself. I don't know what happened to you when you were abroad, but I've seen men and women with their lives ruined by trauma—mood swings, fear, night terrors, nightmares. It's not something that can be ignored.'

He nodded. 'I know.'

She leaned forward in earnest. 'Then you must do something about it! Do you want another night like this one? You must have woken the entire building, screaming. It was awful—it sounded like someone was hurting you.' She paused. 'I can't bear the thought of you being hurt.'

He smiled his thanks, and for a moment she thought that he might reach out and take her hand. But whatever internal battle he was fighting stopped him from doing so.

'You're right,' he said. 'I've been like this for a while. I need to make it stop.'

'So, will you get yourself a counsellor? I

know of a good therapist in Nairn I can recommend you to.'

'You do, huh? Now, how is it that *you* know
a good counsellor?'

She smiled, not allowing herself to give
anything away. 'It's my job to know who to
recommend people to.'

'Your job?'

Jess nodded. 'Yes, my job. Now, you've got
a big day tomorrow—a full clinic. You need
to get some sleep.'

'So have you.'

He didn't know about the decision she'd
made. The phone call she'd had with Jack,
apologising for doing so, but asking to take
some time off for 'a health matter'. Jack
had been curious, of course, but had read-
ily agreed as long as she kept him informed.
She'd told him she would be in the next morning to explain fully. It wasn't a meeting she
was going to enjoy.

'I won't be in clinic tomorrow. I'm taking
some time off. Something I'd already booked
before I started,' she lied.

She just felt that she couldn't work right
now. Not until she'd found out if she was safe
to practise. And that would mean talking to
Jack. That would mean talking to her con-

sultant on the mainland and she wasn't sure she wanted to do that over the phone. She needed to go and see these people—sit down with them face to face. Her consultant would probably want to run some tests.

Since walking out on the procedure with Adam, her arm had spasmed two more times, and each time it had happened her heart had sunk with dread. If this was the first sign of the Huntington's beginning to affect her, then it was beginning earlier than it had with her father—and that was a scary prospect.

If she could keep this news from Adam, then that was what she would do. No point in telling him if it was something else. No point in worrying him before it was absolutely necessary.

'Oh. I didn't know,' he said.

'Well, you do now. So, let's get you back into bed.'

She blushed, turning away from him so he couldn't see her face. She'd never thought that she'd be leading Adam to his own bedroom. And if she had ever dreamt of it, it wouldn't have been like this.

'Yes, ma'am.'

She pushed open his bedroom door and noticed the tangled sheets on the bed, where he must have thrashed and fought his way out of his bad dream. She stood to one side, feeling awkward, not sure what to do next. She knew she didn't feel right leaving him— because what if it happened again?

Adam looked at her intensely. 'Would you stay? You could lie next to me on the bed. There's plenty of room.'

She looked from Adam to the bed, imagining herself lying next to him, as she often had in her dreams. How could she resist?

'Sure. At least until you fall asleep, if that's what you need.'

'Thanks.' Adam clambered into bed first, pulling the sheets over himself and settling his head on the pillows.

Jess felt awkward as she walked around to the other side of the bed, removing her robe and lying down beneath the sheets, laying her head on the pillow next to his, facing him.

'Do you want to talk until you fall asleep?'

'No. This is good. Just having you here beside me. I feel better.'

She smiled, glad. 'Goodnight, Adam.'

'Goodnight, Jess.'

She liked the way he was looking at her. Loved the way his eyes shone in the darkness of the bedroom. The way the shadows

fell across his face. The way it made her feel
to lie next to him. She told herself to soak up
the moment, because when would she ever
have this again? The fact that he'd asked her
to stay made her feel...*wanted. Needed.*

Adam reached up to stroke her face and
her breath hitched in her throat as his fingers
stroked delicately across her cheek, down her
jawline, his thumb brushing over her bottom
lip. He was looking at her mouth so intently!

Her heart was beginning to hammer loudly
in her chest. Could he hear it? Could he tell
her pulse was racing? Feel the heat in her
cheeks? The anticipation of what he might
do next was making her body tingle.

His hand slipped beneath her hair at the
nape of her neck and he moved closer to press
his lips to hers.

Jess closed her eyes in blissful response.
She knew she shouldn't be letting this happen. But the fact that she'd told herself that
this was forbidden just made it all the more
exciting, and she knew she didn't want to
stop.

What was one night? What was one connection? Was she going to be a nun for the
rest of her life? No! So why not? Why not do
this with him?

She liked him. Fancied him. They had a connection and she knew his secrets. They'd grown close lately and he was starting to mean so much to her. They could be adults about this. And, dammit, if her disease was going to rear its ugly head now, then this might her last chance to enjoy being with a man whilst her body still felt under her own control. And she would take it right now!

Jess reached for his body, pulling him closer, feeling the heat of his skin beneath her fingertips, the hardness of his muscles, the thrilling feel of his arousal against her urging her on, telling her she needed this. She savagely cast aside her doubts and allowed herself to be free of her usual constraints. Free of the tight rules she'd given herself. This was not a time for those. This was a time just for her and Adam.

He manoeuvred himself above her, his hands raking over her body, and she arched towards his touch, revelling in every sensation she could feel. This was how a body was supposed to work. This was what she was meant to have if the world was fair.

He peeled her tee shirt over her head and cast it to one side, his hands enveloping her breasts, squeezing and rubbing her nipples to peaks, and it just felt so damned good!

'Adam…' she breathed, her lips grazing the skin of his neck, his jaw, before they found his mouth again, her tongue meeting his.

She wanted to devour him and to be devoured herself. To lose herself in this. All the tight tension she'd been feeling for such a long time without release was now being freed. She wasn't thinking about her arm, she wasn't thinking about the future, she was just experiencing the *now*.

As his exploring fingers reached down and slipped inside her underwear, finding the sweet spot that had been so long ignored, she gasped and drew him tighter against her, urging him on.

She didn't want this to end.

CHAPTER NINE

ADAM WOKE EARLY to the sound of birdsong outside. He was feeling good, content, safe, and it took him a moment to realise why and remember that he hadn't spent the night alone. He opened his eyes, hoping to see Jess still there, her hair across his pillows, to watch her as she continued to sleep. But he saw with immense disappointment that she had gone.

When had she left him?

How was she feeling after their shared night?

He sank back against the pillows and hoped she was all right. What had driven him to do that last night? To take their friendship and push it in another direction entirely? Had he just been seeking a distraction? Something joyful that felt good after the horror of his nightmare? Had he simply sought consolation in her arms? Did that mean he had *used* her?

He hoped not. He had genuine feelings for her. He was attracted by her compassion, her sensitivity, her caring. Physically, he'd been attracted to her since day one… But he was her mentor, and he had sought a physical release with her without considering what it might do to them as friends.

He felt closer to her, that was for sure, and it had been so good between them! As if he'd found the yin to his yang. They'd matched each other perfectly.

Guilt almost swallowed him as he thought that last thought. He hadn't been with anyone since Anoush, and now that he had what did that mean? That he was moving on? Forgetting her? Leaving her memory behind?

No. That could never happen.

It had felt good to be holding someone again. He'd never thought that he would, but Jess had felt so right against him. The scent of her, the feel of her…her hair spread over his pillows. The way her face had looked as she'd gasped his name, her lips open as she breathed against him, the heat of her breath against his neck…

Selfishly, he just wanted to put that moment in his mind and treasure it. Keep it. She'd felt so soft and warm and right.

He sat up in bed, swinging his legs so that his feet were on the floor. Should he go and knock on her door? See how she was? Make sure everything was still okay between them before he headed into work? He didn't want there to be any awkwardness between them.

He sat for a moment, trying to figure out how he felt with her gone.

It was funny how a man could change in so short a time. When his father had first asked him to work with her he'd almost been a little bit resentful at being put with such a junior doctor. But then he'd got to know Jess...got close to her.

And now he was finding himself missing her when she was gone. Missing her smile, missing her laugh, missing the way she made him feel when she was around... He missed how wonderful it felt to be close to her.

Something was happening between them, and although he was fighting it, part of him wanted to roll over and give in.

Jess was an amazing person. The way she cared for him, the way she put herself out— as she had last night, coming down to make sure that he was okay, to check on him. Not many people would have done what she had, and he was grateful for her friendship.

He remembered again how it had felt to hold her against him and wondered what it might feel like to hold her properly and know that she was his for ever…

She'd got no sleep at all, lying in Adam's arms for an age, her mind in turmoil, before pulling away and getting dressed as his breathing became steady and she knew he was in a deep sleep.

She'd thought about leaving a note, but hadn't been able to think of what to put. What did you write after you'd just had the most sexually exhilarating night of your life with your work mentor and friend? What would sound casual, as if everything was okay, when in reality her mind was brimming with crazy thoughts and feelings and she simply didn't know how to think?

Allowing herself to get carried away like that…what had she been thinking? It had made all this so much more complicated than it needed to be.

But she had craved his touch last night. She had needed him so badly—had needed to know what it felt like to want so badly she thought she might burst. To be touched as if she had something to give. To be caressed as if she had value and worth—things she'd often felt lacking in since her diagnosis.

She'd thought herself capable only of hurting people if she got involved with them, but it turned out she was still capable of giving pleasure. Of being a woman underneath the label of her illness.

She had come to work early, knowing that Adam might try and find her before he left for work, and she wasn't sure she could face him right now, knowing that last night had meant more to her than she might ever have believed, and knowing that in her heart she wanted more of it and that it would be torture if this was as far as it could go.

She also knew that Adam would be in the clinic this morning, so she'd loitered in the female changing rooms, taking a shower and getting changed before going the long way round to Jack's office.

She was nervous. Extremely nervous. Because what he was about to say would change the course of the rest of her life. If he said that he thought it was the beginning of Huntington's showing itself then she would have to rethink what she would do. She'd hoped to be a doctor for a lot longer than this. She'd hoped that by the time she started showing symptoms progress might have been made in Huntington's research.

Only there'd been nothing. Nothing that was useful to her right now, anyway. There was going to be some research in the future, screening the entire genome for new drug targeting, but that would take a heck of a long time yet.

Ideally, what she needed was for Jack to say that in his opinion this was just a blip—an intermittent tremor, perhaps even a trapped nerve. The spasms didn't *have* to mean it was Huntington's chorea. She needed him to say that he would support her. Take care of her. Liaise with her consultant on the mainland.

Judy greeted her with a bright smile and she forced a smile back. 'I'm just going to have a quick word with Jack. He's expecting me. Does he have anyone with him?'

'Not at the moment. And he's just got off the phone, too. You go right ahead.'

She stood outside Jack's office and stared at his nameplate on the door. Was she making a mistake, telling him about this? He was Adam's father, but he was also her boss, and she knew she should have told him about the Huntington's at her interview, or even on her application. But she'd deliberately left it off, and she knew that made her in breach of the promises she'd made to reveal everything that mattered to her employer.

To go in as a patient, and not as his employee, would be—*was*—frightening.

Jess raised her hand, paused for a moment, then knocked. She sucked in her breath until she heard Jack say, 'Enter.' Then pushed open the door.

'Jack? Is it okay to have that chat with you now?'

He must have seen something etched into her face, heard something in her tremulous voice that told him that this was not just another chat with his favourite new doctor. He looked at her and nodded, then picked up his phone and told Judy that he was not to be disturbed.

Jess closed the door behind her and slipped into the seat opposite him. This room had brought her comfort the first time she'd come here. The pale taupe colour on the walls... The framed certificates... The bookshelves filled with medical books... The windowsill with the family photos...

There was one she hadn't noticed before, of Jack and Judy together, cutting a cake at some party. A wedding anniversary? And on the desk there was a snow globe of the Loch Ness monster that made her smile nervously. It seemed to sit there in expectation, waiting for her to do her thing. To reveal her big secret.

He could fire her, if he wanted to. She'd not been honest. She didn't know how to start this conversation. She didn't know how to voice her greatest fear. To tell him about the thing that could change everything—her life and her future on this island. It could all be over in seconds, and whatever she thought might be happening between her and Adam would be over too, before it had even begun.

Jack stared at her. She could feel his eyes upon her, assessing, wondering. But then he showed her why he was such a great doctor. He leaned forward and asked, in the softest of voices, 'What's wrong?'

She felt the pain of tears prick her eyes, but as her vision became blurry she managed to meet his gaze, nod her head and say, 'There's something I haven't told you.'

Her voice was almost a whisper...

* * *

When Adam arrived for work he saw he had a long list of patients for the general practice clinic. He was looking forward to it after having such a good sleep. His best sleep in over a year, because Jess had stayed with him.

His mind kept wandering to ways he could make it happen again, but all of them involved a relationship of some kind and he was too terrified to go down that route.

But he really liked Jess. He was developing feelings for her, he could tell.

I need to keep them under some sort of control!

But how could he when he was so worried about her? She was constantly on his mind and something was clearly bothering her.

Was it him? Did she harbour feelings for him too, but, because she knew him to be a fragile, broken thing was holding back from him, not sharing with him? Did she think he already had enough going on?

He knew he had a problem, but it was one that he'd managed on his own for over a year now, and he'd thought it was something that only bothered him on occasion so didn't need constant attention.

It was the occasional panic attack. The occasional nightmare. Mostly he didn't have them, and he'd managed to hide them from everyone. Even his parents had no clue. They knew what had happened to him, but they didn't know about the *effects* of it.

Perhaps Jess thought that if he couldn't be honest with himself he wouldn't be honest with her? Was that why she wouldn't share with him whatever it was that was going on with her? Even if she had shared his bed last night.

There was definitely something—something that she wasn't telling him. But he knew it was unfair of him to expect her to reveal all when he was hardly capable of doing the same. They'd bared their bodies, but not their souls.

Imagine what it might be like if we did...

She was there for him. The way she had come to his flat in the middle of the night, concerned for his well-being... It had made him feel a little embarrassed at first—the fact that she had heard him cry out, that she was aware of his bad dreams and how they were making him suffer.

But he knew she was not the one who'd made him feel embarrassed—that was all his own work. The dent to his pride that he felt as a man was stupid—he knew that—but it didn't stop it from being there.

He'd been so used to looking after himself, to standing alone, to *being* alone, that he wasn't sure how to deal with someone who was so intently looking out for *him*. He'd had it working on the frontline, sure, but after the ambush, and the death of his colleagues and Anoush, he'd told himself never to expect that level of support again. Not from people who didn't know him.

He'd known his parents would be there, of course, but not Jess. And yet here she was, caring for him, worrying about him, when clearly she had something going on in her own life. What could it be?

For a brief moment last night they'd both been able to forget the real world and had existed in a simple world of physical pleasure, but he knew that could never be enough. It was fun, yes, but not something that could be sustained with any meaning.

The first patient to come into his clinic was a young girl of nineteen, Cara O'Leary. She was clutching onto her bag as if it were a lifeline, and not quite meeting his eyes as she sat down in the seat opposite him.

He waited for her to settle before speaking.

'Hello, there. I'm Dr Campbell—how can I help you today?'

'I'm…er…pregnant.'

The fact that she wasn't smiling, or beaming with happiness, or doing cartwheels around the room, suggested that maybe this announcement—this situation—was not something that was welcome. However, he often found it was best to wait and let people tell him how they were feeling, rather than making assumptions.

'Okay. How many weeks?'

She shrugged, fiddling with the strap of her bag. 'I'd guess at about five or six. It's early days.'

'And were you trying to get pregnant?' he asked gently.

Cara shook her head. 'No. I wasn't. I can't have children.' She looked down at the floor, biting her lip. 'I'm not meant to.'

Adam passed her a tissue from the box on his desk to help her dry the tears that he could see were about to fall. As she gathered herself, he took the time to have a delve into her medical history. And that was when he realised that poor Cara had congestive heart failure, which meant that if she were to get pregnant the condition would put such a strain on her heart that she most likely would not survive.

'I see. When did they discover your heart issue?'

She sniffed, dabbing her eyes. 'Two years ago. I'd always had problems—my mitral valve was replaced, and I had a significant cardiomyopathy before I went into heart failure. My consultant told me not to get pregnant, that the risk would be too great. The blood volume alone created by pregnancy would put too much strain on my heart.' She sobbed.

Adam sympathised. To be put in such position as this was awful. And she was so young. She'd probably had dreams of having a family one day, only to be told that to do so would put her own life at risk. And now she'd got pregnant by accident and knew that it couldn't continue.

'I understand,' he told her. 'Who's your consultant?'

He looked back at her notes, pulling up a letter from the mainland hospital that had dealt with her cardio condition. The letter was signed by a Mr Porter.

'Do you want me to contact Mr Porter and

just double-check with him before we arrange anything?'

She shook her head. 'I know what he'll say. We've been through this so many times. I know what I have to do. Besides, I'm already feeling breathless. It's already affecting me. I have to go through with a termination.'

'Normally I would suggest you talk to someone before making such a big decision. Do you have support from others? The father of the child?'

'Yes, I'm lucky that way, I guess. He's in the waiting room, if you want to speak to him, too. But I need this to be over. The longer I'm pregnant…'

'Of course. Considering your unique situation, I can do that. But the fact that you've mentioned you're breathless already is concerning me—would you mind if I quickly examine you?'

Cara shook her head.

Adam completed a basic examination, spending a lot of time listening to her heart and lungs with his stethoscope. Her blood pressure was a little raised, and her pulse faster than he would have liked it to be— though that could just be from the stress of the situation that she was in. He got her to do a breath test, to check her lung capacity, and the results were not great.

'All right, I'm happy to get you booked in, but I'd like you to be kept under strict observation whilst you have it done. Obviously your heart is already under strain, and the stress of the procedure will add to it. Considering all of this, I'm not sure that we should carry out the procedure here in the hospital. I think, instead, we'll take you over to the mainland and have it done there, where you can be observed properly by a cardiologist. But I'm going to admit you here, straight away, before we arrange the transfer.'

She looked disappointed. 'I thought that might be the case. Okay, let's do it.'

'All right. I'll get you admitted. The request will go over to the mainland today, and because it's urgent I'll ask that they transfer you by this evening. You should get someone to pack you a bag and be ready to go with you, because I want this to happen sooner, rather than later.'

Cara nodded. 'Good.'

'You know, just because this is what you expected, you still need to take some time to process what's happening here. I'd highly recommend some counselling.'

He felt a little disingenuous, suggesting this when he himself had fought against counselling all this time, but in this situation he felt strongly about it. Cara was terminating a pregnancy. She was losing a baby that at any other time and place might have been welcome and loved, cherished and adored. The dreams she might have had for her life had already been changed by her health situation. She might benefit from being able to talk about how this loss had affected her.

After Cara had left the room, closing the door behind her gently, Adam sat for a moment, thinking about her situation as well as his own. He had suggested counselling to his patient, knowing that she would benefit from it, so why was he fighting it for himself?

If he was being honest, he knew that counselling was the right thing. He was suffering from PTSD—he had to admit that. Because until he accepted that he had a problem he couldn't fix it, and Jess had begged him to give it a try. Perhaps if he did, he might just get the perfect night's sleep that he dreamed of achieving. Perhaps it would help him put into perspective exactly what had happened during the ambush and he would be able to accept surviving when others hadn't?

Adam sent through the request for Cara's transfer and procedure first, then looked up the directory of counsellors on the mainland and picked up the phone to make an appointment for himself. He felt nervous doing so, but he also knew that it was the first step in the right direction.

Jess would be proud. He wanted to call her and let her know what he had done. He wanted to hear her voice, wanted to share with her his news. But he knew he had a whole list of other patients to see first.

CHAPTER TEN

JESS FINISHED HER tea and placed the cup and saucer on Jack's desk. 'Thank you for listening. I appreciate you taking time out for me.'

'I will always have time for you, Jess. I'm glad you've told me. I wish you'd told me earlier, so that I could have put some things in place to support you, but…'

'I was worried you wouldn't give me the job, and I wanted to come here so badly.' She felt awful.

'I would never have turned you down because of the Huntington's. But I know now, and we can do something about it.'

She smiled and let out a deep breath. She'd shared her greatest fear with him and he'd been wonderful—had even run a series of physical assessments. The spasms still came, most often when she held her arm in a certain position. And because of this finding Jack had suggested that it might not be the beginning of Huntington's, as she feared, but something completely benign that she shouldn't worry about.

To be on the safe side, and worrying about the safety of her patients, Jess had asked if she could take a week out. That way she could monitor the situation over the next few days, speak to her neurologist, adjust to what was happening and keep an eye on the spasms.

She didn't feel right about practising as a doctor knowing that her arm or hand could spasm at any moment. It would be embarrassing for her, as well as disturbing to any patient who noticed—especially if she was in the middle of a procedure or even the delivery of a baby. What if she dropped the baby? That would be awful! Horrifying! Not to mention downright dangerous. She couldn't justify putting anyone in danger until she knew for herself, for sure, just what was going on.

If this was just an intermittent spasm it was probably caused by tiredness. Or all the nervousness of her attraction to Adam and spending time with him keeping her on edge. Including sharing his bed last night!

She wasn't worried about leaving him in the lurch. He probably wouldn't miss her anyway. Maybe he was even having regrets about last night. Had he woken with a clear head and realised they'd both made a mistake? He'd appreciate the distance, and he'd appreciate not having a shadow reminding him about the need to get help for himself. He probably thought she sounded like an annoying stuck record. Besides, if she was lucky, this could all be nothing and she wouldn't have to tell him anything.

As if Jack could read her thoughts, he leaned forward on his desk. 'Have you told Adam about what is going on?'

Horrified at the idea of telling Adam anything about her Huntington's, she shook her head. 'No. It doesn't feel right to tell him. And what's the point of saying anything unless I know for sure?'

'That seems fair.' Jack sighed. 'I understand you're in a difficult situation. Maybe later? When you know more?'

She looked Jack straight in the eye and nodded. 'Thank you.'

Jack looked uncomfortable. 'I care for you, Jess. My wife cares for you, too. We knew you'd lost your father, and now I know why and how. You're in a difficult position—I appreciate that—but I want you to know just how much you have our support.'

There was a sudden knock at the door just before it swung open and Adam appeared, as if summoned. He looked as if he was about to say something to his father, before he noticed that there was someone in the room with him. He turned to apologise for interrupting the conversation and then obviously realised just who his father was with.

A broad smile broke across his face. 'Jess? I didn't know you were at the hospital today. I thought it was your day off?'

Seeing him standing there, and with his father's wise words ringing in her ears, Jess stood up quickly and gathered her things. 'It is. I was just leaving.'

'Are you all right?'

'Everything is fine!' She glanced at Jack, knowing he would keep her secret.

Everything wasn't fine, and she wanted to tell Adam. But she just wasn't ready yet. Perhaps in a week? After she'd had time to monitor herself, to see if her life was beginning to change in the way it had been predicted.

Jack's empathetic smile made her feel as if she was being complicit in a crime. Standing

there in front of Adam and claiming everything was fine.

But news like hers deserved some sort
of delicate approach. Soft lighting, relax-
ing music in the background. It needed to
be built up to and gently broken, not just an-
nounced in an office doorway before she
disappeared for a week. Not right after the
wonderful night they'd shared. She wanted
to hold on to that memory for a while—not
have it ruined by an announcement that she
didn't want to make.

'I've got something to tell you,' Adam said,
touching her arm to stop her from rushing
off.

'Have you?'

She looked at Adam and could see the
confusion on his face as he tried to read her
nervousness. She so desperately wanted to
explain to him what was going on, but until
she knew for sure—for herself—there was no
point in telling him anything. The thought of
telling him was already terrifying, so she was
in no hurry to tell him right now.

'I think you'll like it. Let me tell you at
dinner tonight.'

Jess glanced at Jack once again. Adam
mentioning dinner would make Jack think

there was something going on between them. How could she tell him that they were just friends when she knew in her heart that she wanted to be so much more? If she said that out loud—*We're just friends*—it would be like admitting to herself that she was the one thing with Adam that she didn't want to be.

Just friends.

She wanted more. Dreamed of more. Especially after what they'd shared. Being with Adam physically had made her realise all that she was shutting herself off from, and that had hurt. But she couldn't have it.

'I'm sorry, I don't think I'll be able to make dinner.'

She knew she would be disappointing Adam. And she was desperate to know what his news was. But she comforted herself with the fact that she needed to take this week away. After this week, she would know for sure if these spasms were something simple or the start of something she didn't want to even contemplate.

She had to get to the mainland. See her neurologist. Get the facts.

She saw confusion in Adam's eyes—and did she see something else there? Was that *hurt*? It surprised her, startled her, and she looked away as she tried to process it.

'Are you sure?' he asked. 'Because you said last night that—'

She held up her hand to silence him. Whatever would Jack think now? Adam had mentioned that they'd been together *last night*... She didn't dare look at the older Dr Campbell. She could only guess what he was thinking and feeling...

'I'm taking the week off and I'm not sure I'll be at home; I might have to go to the mainland. Now, if you'll just excuse me...?'

She grabbed her things and quickly moved past him, feeling tears prick at the backs of her eyes as she did so.

Why did life have to be so complicated? Why couldn't it be simple, just for once? Why did it have to be so painful?

'You two were together last night?' his father asked curiously.

Adam turned and glared at his father, ignoring his question. 'What was that all about?'

His father looked away purposefully and sat down behind his desk, reaching for some paperwork.

Adam felt his irritation rise. He knew when people were hiding things from him, and he could clearly see that his father knew something that Adam did not.

'What's going on? Is there something wrong with Jess?'

Jack shook his head, refusing to make eye contact until Adam leaned forward over his father's desk.

'If there's something going on, then I need to know about it.'

'There's nothing I can say.'

'Why? Has she told you not to?'

'It's complicated, Adam.'

'Why is it? It seems very simple to me. You know something, and you should share it with me. Jess is my friend and I care about her. If there's something wrong then I should know.'

His father looked back at him, almost imploring him with his eyes not to push the point.

And that was when Adam had a moment of clarity. 'It's not because you don't want to, is it? It's because you *can't*.'

Jack leaned back in his chair and stared at his son regretfully.

'Is it because of some kind of employer/employee confidentiality?'

'That's right.'

'You do realise I could just go straight onto a computer and look up her records right now?'

'You could try—but you won't find anything. There's nothing on the system. You know that the nature of where we live means that I have always protected the confidentiality of my staff. Individual records are kept on *my* computer and my computer alone. They're encrypted and password-protected. You won't find anything on Jess.'

'You must be able to tell me *something*. Is it serious?'

Jack let out a heavy sigh. 'You need to talk to Jess. If anyone is going to tell you about what is going on, then it needs to be her.'

Adam sank into the chair opposite his father and thought carefully. Something was most definitely going on. Something to do with that spasm. Something that was making her take the week off. What could it be?

His brain raced through all the possibilities he could think of. Medical conditions, other causes of spasms…

Apart from that one moment when her hand had shaken Adam had assumed that Jess was absolutely fine. In good health.

Last night she'd been...amazing! He couldn't think of any other symptoms that she might have shown. So what was so scary that she couldn't tell him?

He resolved to find out.

It felt strange not to be going into work. Jess was used to keeping herself busy, helping people out, studying, doing research, working at the hospital, seeing patients...

Suddenly to have free time left her feeling a little bit lost. Logically, she knew that she should use this time productively, to get on with things that she had been putting off. Some reading, maybe enjoying the baking that she used to love so much... Simple things, but things she had put to one side to focus on her work.

She wasn't used to focusing on herself.

But she knew she wouldn't be able to concentrate on anything until she'd got this spasm thing sorted. It could be something simple, but if it wasn't...

More than anything she dreaded it being the start of her disease, but after that her greatest fear was telling Adam.

She really didn't want him to know. Why ruin things for him? She knew he liked her.

It was very much mutual, and he'd become a close friend in a short period of time. It was almost as if they'd known each other for ages. But he had enough on his plate. Did she really need to burden him with this, too?

The only way she could get away with not telling him would be to leave the island and go and work somewhere else. Randomly, she brought up a job site for medical personnel and checked out what vacancies there were.

There were plenty. Aberdeen, Edinburgh… Or something further south… London. Dorset. Brighton. She could go anywhere—but who would want her? With Huntington's? She couldn't imagine anyone wanting to take her on, no matter how supportive their occupational health department was.

She narrowed her search to obstetric opportunities and found a part-time position, just Mondays and Fridays, at a hospital in Cardiff. There was another in Northampton. She could go! Leave Adam with nothing but fond memories of her.

Would they take me on even part-time with Huntington's?

But should she take this opportunity now that she'd had this scare? She'd come to the island seeking the happiness she'd experienced here with her father, but what if that had been the wrong thing to do? What if the spasm she'd experienced was a wake-up call? Telling her to do what she wanted to do before she ran out of time? Perhaps she should apply for an obstetrics fellowship? Live her life! Live her dream before it all came crashing down?

And that was when she realised she'd made a huge mistake by coming here to Thorney. She'd headed back into her past, chasing ghosts, when she should have taken a step towards her future!

What have I done?

The 'Apply Now' button glowed a soft blue at her. Enticing her. Prompting her. What did she have to lose? She could have so much to gain. Yes, it would be difficult to say goodbye to Adam, and of course Judy and Jack, but it would probably be a good thing.

She'd allowed Adam and his family to get too close. Had allowed them into her heart. She'd begun to yearn for things. Family, love, affection, Adam's arms wrapped around her... All the things she should not dare to dream of. Not without ripping out their hearts—and she could not do that in good conscience. Adam's parents wanted grandchildren. She couldn't give them that if Adam got more involved with her. She'd not just be ruining his life, but their dreams, too.

Outside, the sun shone brightly. She would go for a walk soon, she thought, but first she would fill out an application. She'd probably never hear back, but what if she did?

Biting her bottom lip, she hit the button and began to fill in the online application form. Her stomach was doing triple somersaults at this turn of events, but she kept telling herself that *if* this had just been a spasm, and *if* she got accepted, she might soon be doing her dream work. Training in obstetrics. Following her passion. Being what she'd always wanted to be!

She worked through it, taking time and care over the personal statement and on 'Extra Information' page. By the time she was done she'd been in her hunched position so long, concentrating so hard, that her back and shoulders hurt.

A walk in the sea air and the coastal breeze would blow away the cobwebs and the feeling of guilt that she'd had since walking away from Adam without an explanation—not just in the middle of the night, but also in his father's office.

She grabbed her keys and a bottle of water and headed down to the coastal path. There was a trail, called the Thistle Walk, that would take you around the entire perimeter of the island—around twenty-three miles in total.

If Jack was right, and this was the start of her Huntington's, then physical tiredness would aggravate the chorea. And hadn't she taken this week off so that she could either confirm or deny the onset of her disease? Jess didn't like uncertainties. That was why she had taken the diagnostic blood test in the first place—so that she would know. So why not do her best to prove it one way or the other?

She set off. She met a few dog walkers along the way, and took the time to kneel down and greet the dogs, scratching them behind the ears and wishing she had one herself.

She'd never had a dog, simply because her working hours meant it wouldn't be fair to keep it cooped up inside. Doctors didn't often finish on time. Their shift might end at seven p.m., but if something was going on with a patient—a complication, or surgery needed—or a baby hadn't yet been born, then they often stayed on until the patient was sorted. That meant sacrificing their free time. The time to rest and recuperate before the next shift.

This week Jess was determined to enjoy her free time and use it wisely. However, as she walked, she found her thoughts often straying to Adam. How would he react if she went back at the end of this week and told him that she'd decided to leave? Or told him that she had Huntington's? Because those were her two choices.

Both would hurt him. Her too. But she had to think of herself right now—not take on someone else's worries. She needed to be selfish. It was the only way she could get through these difficult times. Reel in her emotions and her sympathies, box up her heart once again and steel herself.

She'd got too close to Adam. Had feelings for him. Feelings that were dangerous. She must lock them away.

She had no doubt that he would be kind either way. Understanding. But that kindness, that affection, would be dangerous. Both to him and her. Adam had things of his own going on. Things that she was not yet a party to. And perhaps that was a good thing? Because the more she knew, the more she'd care.

The more she'd want to stick around and help. But she didn't need to be dragged into Adam's drama, whatever it was. She had enough problems of her own.

Perhaps we should never have met at all? That would make this whole thing so much easier.

Inwardly, she berated herself for being so open to his friendship, for staying in his bed. But what else could she have done? Walked away? She'd wanted to be with him as much as he had wanted to be with her. He'd been her mentor at the hospital—she'd had to spend time with him—and she'd been so determined to be happy here she'd pushed aside her worry about being attracted to him and just got on with connecting with him.

Because she'd thought she would stay here on Thorney for the rest of her life!

Now she knew that choice had been a mistake. And she had no idea how to rectify it. Perhaps, no matter what, she should leave Thorney anyway? It had been a bad decision to come here—she could see that now.

She could only hope that her Huntington's would remain inactive and that her application would get her an interview. She'd been honest on it. Had told them about her hereditary condition. They couldn't discriminate against her for it, but…

She loved Thorney. She loved the people on it. Maybe she even loved Adam a little. Well, that would have to stop. She needed to be sensible and she needed to take the steps that would set her life back on the path that it should have been on in the first place.

Coming to Thorney, being with Adam, the spasm in her arm—all that had made her see clearly for the first time in years.

He was tired. Exhausted. It had been such a long week, and he'd often found himself looking for Jess, so that he could tell her about a patient he'd seen, or a case that he'd had to deal with, wanting to run it by her, see how she would have reacted. But she hadn't been there, and each time he'd realised that he'd felt an incredible sinking feeling in his gut and his heart and known that his feelings for Jess were running way beyond that of a friend…

The thought had startled him at first. It wasn't something that he'd expected. He'd told himself that she would never be anything more than just a colleague. But something had happened. Something that had started when she'd looked out for him when he'd had that panic attack at hearing the gunshots. The way she'd been concerned about him…the way she'd come rushing down to his flat in the middle of the night when his screaming had woken her…the way she'd felt in his arms…

She'd been there for him in a way that no one else knew he even needed.

He enjoyed her soothing presence. Her proximity seemed to calm him, to help him, but it was more than that. It was a strength of feeling that he'd only felt once before, and that had been with Anoush. He'd used to brighten up when he saw Anoush walk into a room, and he felt the same way when he saw Jess each morning. He liked making Jess laugh, the sound of it warmed his heart, and the smile on her face made him feel so good.

After Anoush's death he'd told himself that he would never fall in love with anyone ever again. It was too painful a loss, watching someone you loved die before your eyes. It was too much for one human to have to go through, to experience, to endure.

He'd thought that the grief would overwhelm him, remain with him for evermore, but as each day had passed he'd learnt that it didn't overwhelm him—it became something that he absorbed. It became a part of him. A part that he chose to not focus upon.

It was always there, gently humming away in the background, ready to poke and prod him with its painful touch on occasion, but being with Jess had made his life better. Happier. And he'd begun to realise that being with her, seeing her smile, hearing her joke and laugh, or focus hard on her work, was something that gave him immense joy. And he was missing that.

It was hard to admit to himself that his life had been without joy since Afghanistan, since before the ambush. That for a long time he had been existing in a world of numbness, just going about his business, trying to get through from sun-up to sundown without anything hurting. Meeting Jess had changed all that and now that he didn't have her by his side it was really affecting him in ways that he'd not expected.

He'd tried knocking on her door a couple of times. Popping round when he thought that she might be in, but she'd never answered. At first, he'd been worried. What if she was sick and had passed out in there? He'd even gone to the landlord who owned the building and asked him to check with the spare key. The landlord had let him in and the relief he'd felt at finding the flat empty was incredible. Clearly she was just out and about.

He'd wanted to linger. Had wanted to absorb everything in her flat to see if it gave him any clues as to what was going on, but there was nothing save for a picture of a man he assumed was her father. He knew her father had died. Knew that he'd been her only family.

Now, Adam closed the door on his own flat and sank into a chair, exhausted. He used to enjoy being on his own, but all of a sudden he was filled with the desire to be around people, people who loved him, and so, even though he was tired, he got back up and headed out through the door.

On arrival at his parents' house he knocked before going in and was happily met by his mother, who was in the kitchen, baking some scones. The kitchen smelt wonderful and he settled in, feeling the comforts of home, the comforts of family, and asked the one question that was at the forefront of his mind.

His father might be bound by employer confidentiality, but his mother wasn't. Because she wasn't Jess's boss. She wasn't Jess's doctor.

'Do you know what's wrong with Jess?'

His mother wiped her hands on her apron and settled down in the chair opposite him at the kitchen table. She smiled sympathetically and laid her hand on his. 'You like her, don't you?'

'You don't have to do your matchmaking thing, you know.'

She laughed gently. 'I'm not. It's just obvious. I've seen the two of you together. The light in your eyes, when you're with her. It's nice. I haven't seen you like that since you came home.'

'I worry about her. Something's sent her running for the hills and now I haven't seen her for days. Her personal files are hidden. And Dad won't tell me. But I really need to know she's all right.'

'I'm sure she's absolutely fine.'

He was really beginning to worry. It all seemed so secretive, and he hated that he was the one in the dark. It worried him greatly. He'd finally found someone to care about again and...

'Hasn't Dad said anything to you?'

His mother shook her head. 'He wouldn't

do that even if he wanted to. Speak to Jess when you see her next. I'm sure she will be able to answer all your questions and more. She's a good girl. Open. Honest. Kind.'

'She's never in when I call round.'

'Then perhaps she's busy? Or she's off out enjoying herself. Your father did tell me he'd given her a week off. That she needed it for personal reasons.' She shrugged. 'Perhaps it's something to do with her father? Didn't she say once that it's been nearly two years since his death? Perhaps she's finding the anniversary difficult to deal with. You know how that can be for people.'

He frowned. Maybe his mother was right and he was reading too much into this…

His mother laid her hand on his again. 'When she's back, why don't you invite her round for dinner? Cook her that lasagne you do that's so delicious.'

She stood up again to put on her oven gloves, and opened up the oven to check on her scones. They seemed to be done, nicely golden, and she pulled them out to place them on a cooling tray.

'And if there's anything to tell I'm sure Jess will tell you when she's good and ready.'

'But when will that be?'

'I guess that depends on what's wrong. *If* there's anything wrong.'

She was right. And he knew he did have the capacity to over-worry about things. Perhaps he was blowing all of this out of proportion? Perhaps he was seeing dangers where there weren't any? Perhaps he'd imagined the fear on Jess's face?

Maybe it hadn't been fear, but embarrassment? He was her mentor, he'd been observing her, and she'd probably felt that he was thinking badly about her capabilities, or something.

That has to be it! It can't possibly be anything else, because Jess seems fine!

Adam smiled and thanked his mother. He'd stop worrying and just make sure that he was there for Jess when she came back after her week away. Let her know how pleased he was to have her back.

Because he was missing her.

Missing her so incredibly much.

CHAPTER ELEVEN

JESS'S WEEK WENT QUICKLY. Surprisingly so. And the best part was that she hadn't noticed any tremor since that first day.

No matter how much she pushed herself, and physically tried to tire her body, there wasn't any other evidence of a chorea. Even her neurologist didn't seem too concerned.

It looked as if the spasm that had initially scared her had just been a blip, an unfortunate coincidence—probably brought on by holding her arm in a certain position, trying to remove that lipoma. When she held her arm in the same position to try and re-enact the situation, her arm did, in fact, tremble a little, so it had to be positional.

As the week wore on, she felt more and more delighted by the fact that the spasm did not appear to be the first sign of her Huntington's revealing itself, and she was thrilled when, after her application, she received an invitation to interview for the post as a part-time obstetrics registrar in Cardiff. It made her feel excited about getting back to work, about putting the next stage of her life in motion.

But it would be hard to say goodbye to the island. Heartbreakingly hard. And she couldn't imagine upsetting Adam. The look on his face would be… She simply couldn't imagine it. Would he feel let down? Betrayed? And what would Jack say? And Judy?

But surely she hadn't been here long enough to upset anyone with her departure? And surely they would see that she was simply trying to get the best out of life? Advancing her career in a way that she'd thought she never would?

No. They would have to understand. Coming to Thorney had simply been the wrong direction for her.

She would miss Adam. Incredibly so. And the idea of getting to see him today, being with him, enjoying his company, made her giddy little heart pound away and the butterflies dance in her belly.

It had been so hard to avoid him all week. She'd done the bits and pieces that had needed doing at her flat during the day, when she'd known Adam would be at work. And in the evenings she'd taken herself out to eat, or to watch a play at the local theatre, or to pass the time in a coffee shop, reading a good book. She had not wanted to be at home, knowing that he might knock on her door, because she would have struggled to ignore him.

But, oh, how she had missed him! She couldn't wait to see him again, to work with him, maybe finally have that dinner with him. A goodbye dinner? She owed him that, at least. She'd missed the sound of his voice, the way he smiled, that barely-there dimple in his cheek. She'd missed the glint in his eyes, the way he ran his hands through his hair when he was tired, but most of all she'd missed the way that he made her feel.

She done a lot of thinking in her week off. Thinking about her future and how she could be happy. She'd thought about her past relationships, and what had happened with Eddie, and all that she had learned about herself since.

She might have got a little lost lately, a bit frightened and confused, but she had come out of it with her head clear for the first time in a long time. But at the end of the day it had left her feeling empty and alone, craving a connection, craving a closeness that she had always denied herself. A closeness she had found with Adam. A connection she would have to break.

She and Adam were good together. She really thought they could have something if they tried. But it wasn't worth it. What if Adam fell in love with her and she had to break his heart with her diagnosis? She couldn't make him watch her die. She couldn't make him be her carer. She couldn't bear to deteriorate in front of him day by day.

And her death would not be a quick death. Easy or clean. Her death would be long and drawn out, stretched over weeks, months and years. That was why she couldn't entertain the idea of being with Adam—because she knew what the future would be like, even if he didn't. He would see the future as full of rainbows and sunshine. Getting married, maybe, and definitely wanting to have kids. His mother wanted to be a grandmother so much!

She couldn't offer him that. Ever.

How could she do that to him? Take that happy family future away from him by lumbering him with her useless broken body? How could she put him through that?

She knew that she would have to be honest with him and tell him about her condition. As soon as he knew they would be able to work together without the worry of an unexpected romance. She would effectively take herself off the market so that she could just get on with being his friend for the short time they were together, and it might even make their parting even easier.

Because it was the hiding that she didn't like. The lying. Not telling anyone about her Huntington's had never mattered before, but with Adam it mattered more than anything and she hated keeping it secret.

Adam was at his desk, quietly cursing the computer, which was refusing to let him input the details of his patient's condition, when he heard footsteps behind him. There was something familiar about those footsteps. Light and brisk.

He turned and his face lit up with joy. 'Jess! You're back! How was your week off?'

He tried not to notice how his heart was racing at seeing her again, how his mouth had gone dry, and how his stomach flipped this way and that in his joy. His mind instantly re-played for him the night they'd spent together in his bed. He had to fight the urge to leap up and throw his arms around her and give her a huge squeeze and not let go. At least for a few minutes.

'It was interesting. I did a lot of unexpected soul-searching. How are you?'

'I'm good. But I've been worried about you. I called round a couple of times but you weren't in. Everything okay? We haven't spo-ken since… Well, you know…'

'I'm more than okay. Actually, I'd like to talk to you later, when you have a moment free. Would that be all right?'

He felt concern fill him. 'Sure. I've got these notes to input for my last patient and then we can see the next together, if you'd like? In about twenty minutes?'

'Okay. I've just got to check in with your father first. Maybe I can grab you for cof-fee later?'

'Sounds great. I'll page you when I'm done.'

'Perfect.'

'But everything *is* all right?'

He hated it that he had to keep asking. But he *needed* everything to be all right. He couldn't imagine there being something so badly wrong it would hurt her.

She leaned forward and laid her hand on his, smiling. 'Yes, it is. But I'll talk to you later. I need to go and speak to your dad.'

He frowned. 'Problem?'

She shook her head and he saw she was smiling. Happy. As if a huge burden had been lifted from her. 'No. Just one of those return-to-work things. A catch-up.'

He watched her walk away, feeling so happy that she was back. Everything seemed right again, knowing that she was here, walking these corridors.

He'd not realised just how accustomed he had become to seeing her around. How her presence comforted him in ways he'd never expected to feel. He'd missed her terribly, and had found it so hard to give her the space that she'd clearly wanted this past week.

Knowing that she was just in her flat upstairs, knowing that he could just knock on her door, he had held off from doing so after his attempts earlier in the week, when he'd got the landlord to let him in. It had been *so hard*. Especially when he had something to tell her. Something he knew would make her proud of him.

Waiting to tell her his secret was painful. But he was practising patience—just like his next patient. It was just a minor injury, nothing too concerning, but he'd had to make him wait after spending a lot of time with his previous patient, who'd come in with what he'd thought was indigestion but what had turned out to be angina.

He'd run plenty of tests and had finally sent the patient home with some literature and some GTN spray. Now he just needed to finish off his notes and then he would call that patient through.

He was looking forward to it—working with Jess again.

She was back! And the thought of that just made him feel so good.

Jess couldn't help but smile when she saw Adam again, just as he picked up the next patient's file to see what the minor injury was. He looked so wonderful, standing there in dark trousers and a slim-fit shirt. Deliciously attractive. He was a treat for her eyes, brightening her soul after the difficult conversation she'd just had with his father, telling him that she would be leaving to pursue another career path.

He'd taken it quite well, to give him his due, but she guessed he understood her reasoning, knowing that he couldn't offer her the specialism she wanted at his own hospital.

'Maybe you could come back and be our specialist once you're trained?' he'd suggested.

The file said their patient had suffered a burn to his arm, so she went to the waiting room and called him through.

Mr George Harris was a gentleman in his mid-sixties, and he'd been waiting patiently with an ice pack wrapped around his forearm. Jess escorted him to a cubicle where Adam waited.

'Hello, Mr Harris. We're sorry about the wait you've had. I'm Dr Campbell and this is Dr Young. Why don't you tell us what happened today to bring you in?'

'Two for the price of one, eh? Oh, it was silly. Just something and nothing. But I thought I'd better get it checked out because I have diabetes, and Dr Campbell Senior told me that I have to be careful with injuries in case they don't heal properly.' He turned to look at Adam. 'You look like him. I can see it in your eyes.'

Adam smiled.

Jess guessed that was the thing with living on a small island. Everybody knew everybody.

'And when did you burn your arm?' she asked.

'About six o'clock this morning. I have to get up early to look after my wife. I'm her carer—she's got motor neurone disease and she's in a wheelchair now.'

Jess felt herself stiffen. The poor man! His poor wife! What must that be like? To lose your wife piece by piece, day by day... It was the one thing she dreaded and feared and refused to allow to happen with her own life.

'I see. Go on,' she said, grabbing the overhead light above the bed and positioning it over Mr Harris's arm as she and Adam examined the wound.

'I usually make her some porridge first thing. It's easy for her to eat. And I also take her up a hot water bottle. I'd got the porridge on the stove, and I was just trying to make up the hot water bottle, when something happened with my arm. I'm not sure what...it suddenly didn't seem to have any strength in it. It kind of gave way. I tried not to drop the kettle, but I just seemed to pour the water over my arm. It hurt like a—' He grimaced. 'It hurt a lot. I may have sworn, Doctor. I did what you're supposed to do—I ran it under the cold tap for ten minutes—but the pain was still intense and I could see I'd damaged the skin. I thought I'd better get it checked out.'

'Well, you did the right thing. Who's looking after your wife right now?'

'My next-door neighbours. They're very good in case of emergency. I'm lucky, really. I've got such a broad support network who help me out with Sally.'

'That's good,' said Jess. 'Being a carer, especially to your spouse, can be draining. It's good that you've got people around that you can rely on.'

'I have. But it's not draining at all. I get tired, yes, but I love my wife and I would do anything for her. Knowing that I'm the one who makes her feel better... I'm the one who makes her comfortable... That makes her smile. We have a closeness between us that was never there before. I love her so much... I can't imagine not having her with me. I wouldn't have it any other way. Well, I'd have her healthy, if I could—but that's not to be. It's not the cards you're dealt in life, is it? It's the way you play your hand.'

Jess listened intently to Mr Harris as he spoke, feeling the beginnings of tears at the back of her eyes as he spoke about his wife with so much love. He was a rare man, clearly.

Jess had a lot of respect for carers. For the strength that it must take. The fortitude. It must be a difficult situation, especially looking after those they loved. She couldn't imagine how hard it must be.

Here was a man who was himself getting on in age, who had a medical condition of his own and would probably appreciate an easier life. Enjoying his retirement. Yet here he was, looking after his wife, essentially a full-time job, and still loving her deeply. It would be an honour to treat him and try to make him better.

'Well, let's sort out this burn, shall we?' Adam said, looking at her curiously as she tried to swallow the lump in her throat.

An examination of the skin beneath showed there was some damage to the uppermost layer, but Mr Harris had done the right thing by cooling it beneath cold water for ten minutes. There didn't appear to be any deeper damage, but because of Mr Harris's diabetes they knew they would have to be careful to check for infection.

Adam applied some antibacterial cream and wrapped the wound in a soft bandage, with instructions that he was to have it checked every couple of days by a nurse, and that if he experienced any fever or strange symptoms in the arm he was to come in immediately and not wait.

Mr Harris seemed satisfied, and pleased that he could go home. 'Thank you. I appreciate that.'

'Try not to do any heavy lifting with that arm for a while, if you can. And take care of yourself.'

'I will—don't you worry. Send my regards to your father.'

Adam nodded, and they both watched as their patient left.

Jess cleared away the bits and pieces that they'd used and threw the rubbish in the clinical waste bin.

'Are you all right?' asked Adam.

'Fine!'

'You seemed a little…affected by his story.'

She tried to laugh it off, embarrassed that he had noticed. 'Wouldn't anyone be? All he's doing…looking after his wife…when he should be enjoying retirement and taking it easy.'

Adam shrugged. 'He loves her.'

'But it has to be hard for him! I couldn't do it.'

She grabbed Mr Harris's file to take it back to the doctor's desk and fill it in.

She didn't dare ask Adam if he could.

Now her butterflies had butterflies. She couldn't believe that she was sitting here in the cafeteria, moments away from telling Adam that she was leaving.

She'd told his father at the start of the day, and although Jack had been clearly disappointed he had accepted it and said he would miss her. How would Adam react? After all that they'd been through together? It was a question that had been on her mind ever since she'd made her decision.

She longed to tell him, just so that he would know, so that it would be in the open and she would no longer have to fear getting too close to him.

She'd made a huge mistake by sleeping with him, furthering a connection she now needed to break. But she could let him know just how much she valued his friendship even if she couldn't tell him the rest.

Because she knew the type of man he was. She had no doubt that if she told him the whole truth, once he'd got over the shock, he would want to be there for her, supportive and considerate. His kindness and empathy would trap him.

Her news was not something that was easy to impart to him. It would be different telling someone who wasn't part of the medical profession. Someone who didn't truly understand the ins and outs of what her disease entailed. Someone who didn't care for her. But telling Adam—who was a doctor, who did care, and who would understand exactly what she would be facing—would be a lot harder. Especially as she suspected that his feelings for her ran deeper than those of a friend—as did her own for him.

She sipped from her coffee cup, wincing at the hotness of the drink. He'd told her that he had news for her, too. She briefly wondered what that might be. He seemed happy, so perhaps it would be best if he shared his news first? That way they would be able to enjoy his news, celebrate it, whatever it might be, without the shadow of her own. And eventually her news would be good news, too. Once he'd thought about it, of course.

She saw him the second he walked into the cafeteria. She perked up, sat up straighter, and smiled as his eyes met hers, lighting up with joy. Not for the first time, she wished that they could be something more than they were.

She had not come here expecting to get so tangled up in the life of Adam Campbell, and yet here she was. When she had allowed herself to imagine what life with him might be like, in no part had there ever been the shadow of a degenerative disease looming over them. There had only been happy scenes in her mind. The two of them taking walks together. Walking along the beach with dogs running around their feet. Walking hand in hand, the wind blowing her hair everywhere, so that when he went to kiss her he would have to tuck her hair behind her ears to see her face, touch her face, and gently press his lips to hers.

How it would feel to be just his? Truly his?

It was an unachievable dream, which just made it hurt even more.

She had to force that image from her mind

right now. Because it would never be like that between them. It would never happen.

Once he knew she was leaving, he would stop thinking of how it might be between the two of them, too. And she would content herself with knowing that Adam would one day be happy with someone else, no matter how much it hurt her to imagine that.

Adam was carrying one of the hospital's tablets and he laid it down on the table. 'Can you look after this for me? Just whilst I grab a coffee? Can I get you anything?'

She shook her head. 'No, no. I'm fine. You go ahead.'

He smiled at her and headed back to the self-service area.

She watched him intently, remembering what it had been like to live her life without worrying about the future. Without worrying about the threat of a disease that could attack at any moment and shorten her life. It had been like that once. Before the blood test. But she'd known what she was getting into. And she'd accepted it. But that didn't mean she didn't miss what she'd had before.

Adam arrived back at the table with coffee, a banana and a yoghurt.

She watched as he added a single sugar to

his drink, and then some milk, before stirring. 'How are you?' she asked.

He nodded. 'I'm good. Really good. How about you? I haven't seen you since...since we spent the night together. Is everything all right?'

This was it. He'd set up the moment for her to explain everything. He'd got right to the point and she knew he deserved her honesty.

But she was freaking out. Imagining telling him was completely different from actually sitting in front of him, looking at his beaming smile and doing it for real. Best to hear his good news first...

'Everything's fine! But come on—you told me you had some news. Let's hear it.' She leaned forward as if she was really keen, trying to ignore the racing of her heart, the cold lump of dread in her stomach.

'Okay...' He let out a sigh, a heavy breath. 'I did what you suggested. I found myself a counsellor and I saw her last week. A two-hour session.' He smiled. 'No doubt the first of many.'

'You did?'

This was unexpected! She was so relieved! Now she could leave him knowing he was getting his mental health taken care of. That was a major step for him. A major step towards recovery. She knew it was something he needed, having watched his panic attack beside the car when he'd heard those rifle shots, having heard his screams in the night as he'd wrestled with his terrors.

'That's fantastic, Adam!' She was really pleased for him. 'Really good. How did you find it?'

'I was nervous. And I was sceptical at first. I'm not going to lie. I couldn't see how talking about what had happened would help me. But I thought about what you'd said, and I realised that there was no point in trying to ignore the biggest thing in my life and hoping it would go away if I was still going to be plagued by what was happening in my mind. And I think it did. A little, anyway.'

'That's brilliant! I'm so proud of you for taking that step. I know it must have been hard.'

He smiled. 'It was. Especially when it made me realise that speaking about it out loud was kind of cathartic. And...' he suddenly reached for her hand '...and I want to tell you what happened to me.'

Her heart almost stopped. She wanted to know—of course she did. She'd thought about it a lot, what the details might be, and she'd hoped that one day she would find out the real truth. But now…? If he told her—if she knew—she would be drawn further into his life and it would make it harder to leave.

'You don't have to. Not if you don't want to.'

'I need to. You've been there for me and I owe you the truth.'

'Adam, I—'

He laid his hands upon hers and she stopped talking.

'I was working in a medical centre in Kabul. With International Health…'

She decided to listen. To stop interrupting. Clearly he wanted to tell her something huge, and who was she to deny him the privilege of unburdening himself? And, dammit, she wanted to hear what he had to say. She'd be a liar if she said she hadn't wondered often what had happened to him.

'One day I was part of a large convoy of medical trucks assisting the American army. We were relocating to a new field hospital. But we got ambushed just outside the city of Kabul.'

Jess didn't realise that her hands had become fists. 'Ambushed?'

'The first truck in the convoy was hit. It got blown off the road and took out two of my team. Another one was hit by a rocket launcher. The one I was in.'

He was looking her in the eyes but he wasn't seeing her face. She could tell that he was back there, back in that place, replaying the ambush in his head like an awful movie. She'd not expected to hear this. Any of it. She'd assumed he'd remain private. But now he was sharing all this with her.

To hear he'd been in such danger was upsetting to her. 'Adam—'

He held up his hand as if to tell her that he hadn't finished talking. So she said nothing more. Because she knew he had to say this. And she wanted to hear this.

'Then our truck came under fire—bullets from all directions. We knew we couldn't stay in the truck because there were oxygen canisters in there, and if they went off… So we scrambled out, already bleeding. My leg was almost numb. I knew I was hurt, but didn't know to what extent. I knew it wasn't my femoral artery, so for that I was grateful. There were some large boulders near the roadside, and I thought if we could just get there we'd be away from the danger of explosion and would also be able to take some cover from the gunfire.'

She leaned forward. 'You say *we*? The other medics?'

He nodded. 'I was travelling with a nurse. An Afghani children's nurse. You wouldn't think you'd need a children's nurse in a war zone, but unfortunately you do. Anoush had arrived at the camp the same day as me.'

Anoush. Anoush was a person. When he'd been having his panic attack, he'd cried out the word. But she hadn't known what it meant. Hadn't even known it was a name. She'd thought she was prepared for what he might say next, but she wasn't.

'When you work in places like that—away from family, under intense pressure and danger—your colleagues become your friends, your family. Relationships are formed under extreme duress. You get close very quickly...you spend all your spare time together. Anoush and I were very close.'

Adam looked down at the floor for a moment, before looking up again and meeting her eyes.

'I fell in love with her. Whether it was real love or not, I don't know, but at the time it felt real. I didn't tell my parents, because I didn't quite know if what I had there was what it seemed. You're in a bubble—whether that bubble is pleasant or not. The real world… the mundane day-to-day…just doesn't exist for you there. But I couldn't picture my life without her. So I decided to ask her to marry me. I thought if she said yes, then I would contact my parents and let them know.'

Her breath caught in her throat. Adam had fallen in love. With a nurse in Afghanistan. *Of course.* Why wouldn't he? He was a catch, and he'd probably charmed all the nurses there.

She told herself that she had to accept that because she had nothing to offer him. He wasn't hers. He'd never been hers and never would be. But to actually be sitting there, hearing him talk about the woman he'd loved—well, that drove a dagger into her heart that she'd never expected. It left her breathless, her throat painful with the tension caught there, and she fought back the tears that were threatening to spill.

'Go on,' she managed to say, each word choked out.

'Before we left in the convoy she said yes. She would marry me. And when she said that

I knew I needed to contact my parents and let them know.'

Jess swallowed the lump in her throat. 'But you didn't?'

'No. I figured we'd get to the new field hospital, get everything set up, and once communications were established I'd be able to call home and let them know.'

'But you never got there,' she said sadly.

'No.'

He looked down, but before he did so she recognised the build-up of tears in his eyes.

'Adam… What happened to Anoush?'

He blinked rapidly, sniffed, and took a sip of his coffee.

'We were pinned against the underside of the vehicle. It was on its side. I knew we needed to make a run for the boulders. I asked her if she could make it, but she was more concerned about me and my leg. It was bleeding quite badly, but to be honest I wasn't feeling it too much at that moment in time. Adrenaline is a great numbing agent. I took hold of her hand and told her that on the count of three we would make a run for it. She looked at me then, and it's a moment I'll always remember—because she looked at me as if it was the last moment she would ever see me. I told her we'd make it. I knew I had to make her believe that. I counted to three and then we ran.'

Jess was on the edge of her seat, not quite believing what she was hearing. That he had been in such a situation was terrifying, and she couldn't be more grateful that he was here, safe with her, and not still back there.

'We made a good start. It was a distance of about ten metres to the boulders and I really thought we'd make it, even though all around us we could hear gunfire. We weren't armed, but some of the soldiers travelling with us were, and they were shooting back. We were running and something happened—I don't know what. I tripped, or maybe my bad leg took me down… I let go of Anoush's hand. I hoped she would carry on running for cover, but she didn't.'

He looked Jess in the eyes and she'd never seen sorrow like it.

'She stopped for *me*. Turned. Waited. And I saw her take a bullet to the chest. Right in the heart. I remember looking at her in total shock, watching as she looked down at me before she dropped to her knees. I scrambled towards her, tried to catch her before she hit the ground. She looked up at me, terrified, for just a moment… And then she died.'

Jess sat listening, open-mouthed, trying to imagine herself in such a situation. What would she have done? How might she have reacted in the same situation? Watching the person she loved gunned down right in front of her face. What if she'd been there? What would she have felt to see Adam take a bullet and drop to his knees right in front of her? What would she have done if he had died in her arms?

She didn't realise that tears were dripping down her face.

'It felt like I held her in my arms for ages, but that can't be right. We were in the middle of a gunfight and right out in the open. One of the soldiers grabbed me by the shoulder and began dragging me across the stones. He was yelling, kept telling me to leave her, that we would come back for her later, and he dragged me over to the cover of the boulders. I don't know how I let go, but I did, and I sat behind a rock, not quite understanding what had happened.'

He looked at her more intensely.

'What if the bullet that killed Anoush was

meant for me? If I hadn't tripped, then it would have hit me.'

'You can't think like that. And it doesn't sound to me like that would have happened. You said you tripped, fell. And then you saw her stop and turn around to wait for you. I don't think that bullet was meant for you.'

'But I can't get it out of my head. I feel it was my fault that she died. It was my suggestion to break for cover. I told her when to run and I was the one who tripped. She turned and waited for me. *I'm* responsible for her death.'

Jess took his hands in hers and found that they were icy cold. She rubbed them gently, hoping to warm them, hoping she could show him that she didn't believe he was responsible.

'It wasn't your fault, Adam. You didn't pull the trigger. You didn't start the war. You were trying to save her and she believed in you. She loved you. That's what you need to remember.'

He took her hands in his and turned to look into her eyes. 'You're very kind to say that.'

'It's the truth. Kindness has nothing to do with it. And she died loving you, in your arms.'

He nodded, then seemed to notice that her cheeks were wet. 'You're crying…'

'Am I?' She suddenly felt embarrassed, as if he'd caught her doing something that she should not. 'Sorry, I didn't mean to… Gosh, look at me—I'm ridiculous! I bet I've got panda eyes now.'

'You don't look ridiculous. You look beautiful.'

Jess met his gaze and held it. He thought she was beautiful? She didn't know what to do with that information right now, but she knew she would treasure it in case it was something she never heard from anyone ever again. But to hear it from Adam was…intense. Especially after the night they'd shared.

What was happening here? Was he falling for her? The way she was for him?

Adam reached up and stroked her face, smiling. 'Thank you for listening, Jess. I needed to tell you because you're the one person who's seen through me in all of this. The one person I've allowed to see me.' He smiled. 'You've made me feel like I can begin to move on. Like a weight is being lifted every time I tell the story. I'm even going to tell my parents what happened. I feel… optimistic. And you're a big part of that.'

Her breath caught in her throat. What could she say? All the things she'd wanted to say to him about leaving, about saying goodbye, were impossible to give voice to now. He sat there looking so…so revitalised! So different! The shadow was gone from his eyes. Had he been sleeping better? He said she was responsible for this change in him—how could she tell him she was walking away? Why hurt him when he was finally beginning to heal?

What if he saw this as a step forward for both of them? What if he had expectations of her as more than just a friend? They'd slept together. He'd told her she was beautiful. These were all terrible signs! He would be better off without her, and although it would hurt him in the short run, after a few months he would forget about her.

She pulled her hands free of his. 'I'm glad for you, Adam. And thank you for sharing all that with me. I'm truly honoured.'

'No, thank *you*. Without you, none of this would have been possible—'

'I'm leaving the island.'

She just blurted it out. She couldn't bear to hear him tell her over and over again how important she was to his recovery. She was glad about that, but all it did was taunt her with all the ways she couldn't be important to him. Romantically. Emotionally. Physically. She wanted so much more, but she couldn't have it. She was happy for him, but now it was time to take a step away.

'What? You've only just got here.'

'I made a mistake coming here. I've already spoken to your dad about it. I'm moving back to the mainland to pursue my dream of specialising in obstetrics.'

He looked confused. 'But you'll come back again?'

She shook her head. 'No. I can't do that.'

'But we've got so close!'

Her heart was breaking inside, but she hoped she wasn't showing it. He mustn't know how much he meant to her.

'I know, but we shouldn't have. I'm sorry, Adam. I know it's not what you want to hear. But in the same way that you've made strides forward, so have I. I've done a lot of thinking lately about what I want from life and I can't get it here. It's the wrong place for me.'

'I see. I thought we had something. Maybe I was confused?'

She nodded. Gritting her teeth. Trying not to bawl her eyes out. 'I'm not looking for a relationship. I'm sorry.'

And she slid out of her chair, unable to sit there a moment longer, unable to look at the pain in his face, knowing that she had taken him from happiness to misery in a matter of seconds.

Well, she was doing him a favour.

Better this than a lifetime of misery if he allowed himself to fall in love with her.

She was in turmoil. Her lie—her *life*—was getting more complicated. And at this moment in time she hated her Huntington's diagnosis more than she hated anything in the whole wide world.

CHAPTER TWELVE

ADAM FELT AWFUL. As if his whole world had ended right there and then. How had he gone from feeling so amazing at having Jess back, opening up to her, thinking that it would bring them closer together, only for her to rip out his heart and tell him she was leaving?

This wasn't meant to have happened! He'd imagined sitting there, telling her all his secret as she held his hand, and then once it was over, listening to her as she told him all hers.

It was to have been the ultimate moment of sharing. Of vulnerability. Of openness and honesty. And yet it had all gone terribly wrong.

How had he misjudged this?

Should he go after her? Bring her back? Tell her all over again? Perhaps she'd misheard what he'd had to say? Perhaps she hadn't understood just what he'd been trying to say? Perhaps he'd been wrong in thinking that they were closer than they actually were?

Or maybe she'd sat and listened to him and heard nothing but the ramblings of a broken man? Why would she saddle herself with such a man when he obviously had issues to work through? It was hardly attractive, was it? Plus, she probably felt that he was still in love with Anoush. Still grieving for his lost fiancée.

Yes, he would always feel grief for what he had lost, but he had moved on—and the only reason he had been able to do that was because of her! Had she not heard that part? About how he'd only been able to do all of this *because of her*?

He had tried his *hardest*, his *damnedest*, not to develop feelings for Jess, but he had.

He had even been considering the very real possibility that somehow he had come to *love* her. Which was crazy! But he knew that was what he'd wanted. He'd wanted to take that risk with her.

She had changed his thinking. She had opened his heart to new possibilities, new hopes, a new future, and he'd felt that they were both in a really good place. She was a dedicated doctor and now she'd chosen a specialty that she wanted to focus on. That was good for her. She might need to go to some other hospitals to study, and that would mean moving away from Thorney for a while, but surely he could go with her.

Maybe she thought that he wouldn't want to move away from Thorney because he was getting counselling now? Perhaps all he needed to do was tell her that he could get counselling anywhere? That both of them could find work anywhere.

The week they'd spent apart had been agony, but crucial, because it had given Adam an insight into his feelings for her and he wasn't willing to give those up. Not now that he had them. He'd forgotten how good it could feel, knowing you *had* someone.

No, they hadn't known each other for long, but sometimes you just knew in your soul if someone was right for you. And Jess was.

She'd looked so beautiful this morning. Her eyes bright and shining a honey mahogany behind those silver frames. And the way she'd leaned in to listen to him when he'd first sat down, her face rapt, her joy so clear for him to see, her *love* for him, so blindingly displayed…

He hadn't mistaken that, right?

He had no doubt that she loved him. He just needed to show her that he was okay. That she could depend on him. That he wasn't going to go anywhere.

She'd been left before, hadn't she? By her father. Left alone. Maybe she thought that everyone would do the same? Well, he would prove to her that he was made of sterner stuff.

He needed to talk to her. But maybe not at work.

He wanted to do something nice for her. Something surprising. Something special to mark this day. Perhaps a meal out, somewhere nice? There were a couple of nice seafood restaurants along the harbour. He might ring one of them up and see if he could get a reservation...

He opened up his laptop and looked for the contact details of the restaurant he wanted to try. It had great five-star reviews and the photos looked spectacular.

His mind made up, he rang through to make a reservation.

And then he called a florist.

Jess was finding it hard to concentrate, what with her heart breaking inside her. She'd been so ready to tell Adam everything! She'd built up to the moment, ready for his reaction, ready to tell him that she was all right at the moment and that he wasn't to worry about her, she'd be fine, when he'd hit her with that information about speaking to a counsellor. Told her about what had happened to him in Afghanistan.

He'd watched the woman he loved die right in front of his eyes and it had broken him.

I couldn't put him through that again!

Not when he'd been so happy with his breakthrough moment! That hadn't been the moment to tell him! It wouldn't have been right. He'd done such an amazing thing, admitting he had a problem with PTSD, and she knew how much it took to sit in front of a therapist and open up about your every fear, lay your soul bare.

And now she was expected to work in the primary care clinic for the rest of her shift, and she was finding it hard to remain sympathetic to all the people who came in moaning about a cold, or a sore throat, or a headache, when she had so much more to worry about.

A real disease! With real implications!

Did they not realise how her life was falling apart? No, of course not. That was the role of the doctor—to be human, but not so human that you brought your own problems into the workplace. You were there for your patients, not the other way around. There had to be a professional distance.

She hated herself for being so crabby-minded. Having a cold could make people feel terrible! It could lead to chest infections, or even pneumonia, if they were susceptible. Tonsillitis, laryngitis, bronchiolitis! All that could make someone feel rotten. Stop them from working. Stop them from going to school. And a headache could be any manner of things, so she checked every patient carefully.

It was just…difficult.

But when had anything in her life been easy?

'Mary McMahon?' she called, and smiled when her next patient, a little old lady with silver hair, got up from her chair in the waiting room, clutching a urine sample bottle. Already Jess had some idea of the nature of the presenting complaint, but she tried to not make any assumptions.

Her patient hobbled past her and sat down in the chair, and Jess walked behind her. 'And what's brought you in to see me?'

Mary smiled and placed the urine sample

on Jess's desk. 'I've been feeling a little peculiar the last couple of days and I can't stop going for a wee. Pamela, the warden at my building, suggested I come and see you to check for a UTI.'

A urinary tract infection. A common occurrence in the elderly.

'All right. When you say "peculiar", how so?'

'I don't know. I have this constant urge to go to the toilet, even when there's nothing there, and when there is something there it burns so much I break out in a sweat.'

'Okay. It sounds like a UTI. Let's test this sample, then. When did you do it?'

'Just before I came out. About thirty minutes ago.'

Jess dipped the sample with a urine-testing strip, but the results came back absolutely fine. No sign of any infection.

'That's clear. But it doesn't mean you don't have an infection, and because of your symptoms I'm tempted to give you antibiotics. I will send this off to our lab and see if they can grow anything. Would you object to me checking you internally?'

'No, Doctor. You do what you have to do. I'd rather you got this sorted out. It can't go on like this… I never get through a whole episode of my soaps on the television!'

Jess smiled. If only that could be *her* worry.

She assisted Mary onto the examination table and waited outside the curtain for Mary to undress. Then she went in, washed her hands, gloved up and examined her. Her anatomy was as to be expected in an elderly lady of eighty-one years. Nothing abnormal. Was this some sort of interstitial cystitis?

'We'll treat you with antibiotics, just in case, but I'm going to make a referral to a urologist in case we need it.'

'A urologist?'

'Urologists specialise in this area and they might want to do a more thorough examination if nothing comes back from the urine sample—is that all right?'

Mary nodded and Jess left her to get dressed again, washing her hands and then typing up her notes from the appointment and issuing a prescription for nitrofurantoin.

When Mary came back out from behind the curtain Jess had everything ready to give to her. 'You'll get a letter from the urologist in due course, but I'll ring you when the results come back from the lab and if you don't need the appointment, we can cancel it, okay?'

'Thank you, Doctor. You've been most kind.'

'No problem at all. Take care, Mary.'

'You too, dear.'

And she was gone.

Jess sighed. It was going to be a long day, and it was—

There was a knock at her door.

'Come in.'

Una from Reception came in, carrying a huge bouquet of flowers. 'These just came for you! There's a card, too.'

Jess gasped. The flowers were beautiful! Roses, Scottish thistles, lavender, asters—a real mix of purples and pinks.

'They must be from a patient,' she said, reaching for the card that accompanied them and opening the envelope.

When she pulled out the card, she saw the handwriting and read the message:

Dinner at seven tonight? Shrimpton's?
My treat, to celebrate your news!
Love, Adam x

She couldn't help but smile. How thoughtful he was. How kind. How wonderful! He would make someone an amazing husband one day.

He just won't be mine.

The thought filled her with so much sadness, she had to blink away tears. She'd been so rude, just getting up and leaving the cafeteria this morning. Dropping her bombshell about leaving the island and then just rushing away. He could have been angry about that. He could have been dismissive. But, no, he'd heard what she'd had to say and, although he must be feeling upset and disappointed, he wanted to show her that what she'd said mattered and that he was determined to see the best in it.

He was such a good man.

Why can't I have him? Why?

And then she remembered why. And the sadness and grief hit her all over again.

She couldn't have dinner with him at some posh restaurant. He deserved an explanation. He was trying so hard to make everything right between them—didn't he deserve to know the real reason why it could never work between them? He needed to know—simple as that.

And once he did know perhaps it would be easier for him? Because he'd be able to walk away, like Eddie had. He deserved a happy future. He deserved to give his parents the grandchildren they craved. Healthy grandchildren. He deserved to have a long and happy marriage after all he had been through. He'd watched one woman he loved die right in front of him—he wouldn't want to go through that again with another. Once the implications of all the care she'd need in her later years sank in he would realise there couldn't be a future between them.

It was only right that she called a halt to any ideas or aspirations he might have about them. He was being a good friend. Seeing past her abruptness at the café and trying to hold on to the happiness in the decision she'd made to specialise. He was a special man. A good, decent man. Selfless. Caring. Loving.

If you love someone, you set them free.

Who'd said that?

But she couldn't do it in a restaurant. Having such an awkward conversation in the cafeteria had told her she didn't want any public discord.

Jess picked up the phone and called Adam. When he answered, she kept her reply short. 'I can't do Shrimpton's. But I can do dinner at my place…same time. And thank you. For the flowers.'

She hung up and stared at the phone with a rapidly beating heart.

She was going to do it.

She was going to tell him.

If he could be brave enough to take the next step in life, then so could she.

Feeling nervous about all he hoped to say to Jess, Adam knocked on her front door and waited.

He'd taken a long time to choose what he would wear tonight, when normally that sort of thing barely got a second thought from him. But he hoped tonight would be special. Tonight he would tell Jess how he felt about her, and he figured something like that should be memorable, so it would be better to make it as nice a memory as he could.

He wanted them to be able to look back on it in the future, maybe even with their kids sitting on the floor around them… Wow. That would be crazy. He knew he was racing ahead in what might happen, but he couldn't help himself where she was concerned.

He imagined Jess telling their children that Daddy had turned up wearing a beautiful suit, with a blue silk tie that matched the colour of his eyes, and how impressed she'd been when she'd seen him at her door and had known that the night was going to be a very special one indeed.

He'd never thought of himself as a fanciful person. Or a dreamer. Yet here he was, doing both of those things! Crazy what love could do.

He could hear her moving about inside the flat, and then footsteps as she came to the door and opened it.

She looked stunning! Dressed in a beautiful wraparound red dress and with bare feet. He'd never seen her in make-up before, and tonight she took his breath away. He really had to remind himself to speak, in case she thought he'd become mute!

'You look amazing!'

'Thanks. So do you. Nice suit.'

'I didn't know what you were cooking, so I brought red wine and white wine.' He presented her with two expensive bottles.

'We're having fish, so I guess we'll use the white.'

She seemed a little subdued, and he figured it was probably because she felt a little awkward after earlier. He'd not seen her since she'd left him in the cafeteria. Well, he'd done a lot of thinking since then, and he definitely knew what he wanted from life.

Her.

He leaned in to kiss her gently on the cheek and inhaled the scent of her perfume that was like a meadow. 'You smell nice.'

'Thanks. You shouldn't have gone to all this trouble. Buying the wine...dressing up.'

'It's never trouble where you're concerned. Besides, you deserve it. We've both made huge strides forward in the last week and that deserves to be celebrated. You've chosen your specialty! Big step, Jess!'

She gave a small smile and nervously invited him in as she stepped backwards.

He could smell something delicious cooking. Her flat was filled with heavenly aromas that made him salivate. But he was hungry for more than food. He wanted to tell her everything. Wanted to tell her what she meant to him. Wanted to tell her that he saw a future for them both. Together. That he thought they had something really special. Something he thought could be *amazing*.

She seemed incredibly nervous, but he liked it that she was feeling the same way as him. Maybe not for the same reasons, but she had to have realised that tonight was going to be a big night for them both.

He really wanted to put their relationship on an equal footing and make them official. She probably thought that he was going to happily wave her off at the ferry in a few weeks' time, when instead he hoped to suggest that he would go with her! The urge to tell her right now was incredibly powerful, but he wanted to wait until they were dining.

He hadn't been lying when he'd said they'd both taken big steps. He had never predicted this. His feeling about Jess. After Anoush, he'd thought it would be completely impossible for him to fall for someone else. To risk being hurt again. But Jess had made those things possible.

He wasn't going to question it but go with it. See where it took them. He could see a bright future ahead. And that was something else. He was *planning a future*. It seemed possible now, whereas before he'd come home he'd only seen an existence.

'I've got a few things to do in the kitchen. Can I get you a drink?' she asked, holding up the bottle of white.

'Sounds perfect.'

He followed her through to the kitchen, unable to stop himself looking at her gorgeous figure in that wraparound dress, remembering how it had felt to hold her. The softness of her body. The way her back had arched as he'd brought her to orgasm.

He wanted that again—but more than that he wanted to know that she would be his. Wanted to know that she would be sharing his life, making him laugh, making him smile. He wanted them sharing cosy nights in together, watching movies and eating popcorn, snuggled on the couch. He found himself imagining buying a house with her, hunting for the perfect place, settling down, inviting friends over, being a *couple*.

He couldn't imagine a future with anyone else.

Adam had certainly dressed for a date. The smart clothes, the wine, the way he looked at her…it was almost as if he was trying to court her! But that had to be impossible, right? This was Adam Campbell and she was just Jess. Nobody special. Nobody who could be special to anyone.

It wasn't as if she had anything worth giving him, except friendship. And she'd told him she was leaving the island. Did he think he could come here tonight to change her mind? She hoped not. No matter how much she'd love to stay and be with him, she'd already told him she would be leaving. She didn't want to have to go through such a painful discussion all over again, even if she did owe him an explanation.

That was going to be the hard part.

And yet part of her wanted to enjoy this night. She wanted to wallow in the feelings that being with Adam was engendering. The joy, the easiness, the happiness. Why fight it? Why waste these last happy moments? When else would she get this? This might be her last ever evening with him! Perhaps that in itself was a reason to just take it moment by moment?

She hoped they would make it through to dessert before she told him the truth. At least let the poor man have a decent meal before she ruined everything for him.

'Why don't you take a seat?' she asked him.

'You're sure there's nothing I can do to help out?'

'No. I've got everything under control.' She searched in her kitchen drawer and pulled out the corkscrew. 'Unless you'd like to do this? I'm useless at using these.'

He took it from her gladly, smiling at her, and she had to turn away, grab the oven gloves and check on their main course—something to do to disguise the heat in her cheeks. That way she could blame the oven.

Behind her, she heard the pop of the cork and then the sound of wine being poured into glasses. She turned to accept a glass.

'To new beginnings.' He raised his glass in a toast.

She clinked his glass with hers. 'New beginnings.'

Jess had lit some tealights and floated them in a bowl as a centrepiece for the table. She could see his blue eyes twinkling in the semi-darkness.

Hadn't she wished for this? To be on a date with him? To have one last hurrah? But this was painful. Looking at him right now, knowing that he was hoping for something they couldn't have, knowing that she would ruin any plans he was making for them both… She'd always hated secrets. and she felt terrible at having kept one herself.

'How are your parents?' she asked. A question which was on safe ground.

'They're good. Mum got that twinkle in her eye when I told her I was coming round here for dinner tonight.'

Jess smiled. She could imagine. Judy loved her son intensely, and of course she wanted happiness for him. Wanted to see him settled. With a family of his own. Had Jack told Judy about her Huntington's? She couldn't imagine he'd break that confidentiality. Judy probably still believed her son might have a happy ending with her...

She knew the power of dreams. Of wishing. Of hoping. She'd always imagined her future would hold something else, too. Something like what she had right now. Dinners with a handsome man who cared about her. Loved her. She'd imagined a small house, maybe a cottage. One or two children. A dog. A cat. Chickens in the yard. Growing old with someone. Two grey-haired pensioners still holding hands in the park.

This part right now was painful, knowing it was all just a mirage. This future belonged to someone else. Adam was meant for someone else. Someone who could give him all the things he dreamed of. But he was acting as if he'd already made up his mind. Was this more than a celebratory meal for him? Was he reading something into this relationship of theirs? The thought made her ache inside.

Jess sipped at her wine. She needed to keep a clear head. Besides, she'd never much cared for alcohol. 'I've cooked monkfish. Is that all right?'

'Aye. It's perfect.'

She smiled and put down her glass. 'It should be ready in a moment. A couple more minutes.'

She was nervous. Her belly was filled with butterflies. She almost felt sick. Would she be able to eat? She wasn't sure she'd be able to swallow anything until she'd got this secret out. It was strangling her. She had to do something. Anything.

She grabbed a small knife and stabbed the potatoes to see if they were cooked. They were nice and soft. The food was ready. Thank God! It would give her something to do.

Jess busied herself for a few minutes, draining the potatoes and the baby vegetables and getting the fish out of the oven to rest. She sliced some lemon and began plating up, trying to make the food look pretty—a feast for the eyes. Then she carried the plates over to the table.

'Bon appetit.'

Adam looked up at her. 'This looks and smells delicious. Thank you.'

'No problem.'

She sat down and laid her napkin over her lap, before spearing a piece of broccoli and placing it in her mouth. She wasn't sure where to look. At Adam? Somewhere else in the room? Wouldn't that seem rude?

'This is wonderful. I've not tasted anything better.'

She smiled at the compliment and put down her knife and fork to take another sip of wine. She needed to breathe. Needed to calm herself. Her heart was racing, her mind whizzing at the thought of how he'd react when she finally told him the truth.

He reached across the table to lay his hand over hers, squeezing her fingertips, gently stroking the back of her hand with his thumb.

She almost stopped breathing. She had to stop this. This was too much. It was as if he was reading her mind and doing everything she'd ever imagined him doing. But it couldn't happen. Because Adam didn't know the whole truth.

'Adam…'

If he was going to learn about her condition, then perhaps this was the moment? It would stop him wanting to touch her. Or should she not tell him anything? Could she be a coward and keep her own counsel? Then let him down gently?

It was so hard! She wanted him so much. It was a torture, sitting here like this knowing that as soon as she told him the truth he wouldn't want her. He would pull his hand away, he'd sit back in his chair, and he'd probably just want to get up and leave. What she had to say would be life-changing, for both of them.

Her stomach was churning and she wasn't sure she'd be able to eat anything. However, once she began she realised she could. The food was absolutely delicious, which helped.

Adam started chatting about his father's plans for the cottage hospital and how he wanted to give some of the staff in the Accident and Emergency department more trauma training. She relaxed slightly, glad that he'd taken the conversation on to something easy. Safe. It seemed a good idea and she nodded along, until eventually Adam laughed at himself.

'Listen to me, waffling on. I'm sorry—it's just that I'm nervous.'

'Nervous?' Her stomach did a flip.

'Of you. Of us. Of this. I've been thinking about us a lot just lately, Jess.'

Us. He kept saying *us.* There could never be such a thing!

'Oh?' She heard the tremble in her voice.

'Aye. I have. I really didn't think I could feel this way about another person after what happened with Anoush. I came home to Thorney expecting nothing like this to happen. But it did—it has. And…and I need you to know how special you are to me.'

'Special?'

No. He shouldn't be telling her this! It was agony.

He nodded and reached for her hand once again, unaware that when he did her pulse almost jumped through the roof.

'So special. I… I think I'm falling for you. Falling hard! I can't stop thinking about you, about how you make me feel… And I know you said you're leaving, but… I think you might feel the same way, too. Do you?'

He was looking at her so earnestly. So eager for her answer. And of course she felt the same way. Of course she had fallen hard for him. But it wasn't to be! It couldn't!

'I do care about you, Adam…'

He smiled, relieved.

'But…'

'But what?'

She pulled her hand free of his and tried not to notice the hurt look in his eyes. 'But we can never be together. Not the way I think you want us to be.'

It physically hurt to say the words out loud. To go against everything she actually wanted and sever the ties between them.

There was total confusion in his eyes. 'Why? What's going on, Jess? I thought you felt the same as me. I thought—'

'I'm sorry, Adam. I'm sorry if I made you feel that way. I'm sorry if I made you think that we could be together. Don't get me wrong—I do want that. It's just…'

'Just what?'

She looked into his eyes. Deep into his eyes. He needed to know. He deserved to know the truth. She couldn't hold back any longer. She would tell him and then she would be free, even if it killed her to do so.

'Adam… I have Huntington's disease. My father had it, too. He killed himself because he couldn't bear to make me his carer and let me watch him lose himself day by day— because he couldn't bear to become a victim to this cruel disease. And I can't let that happen to you, either!'

'Jess…'

She couldn't bear it. Couldn't stand the pity in his eyes!

She got to her feet, her chair scraping back loudly across the kitchen floor. 'I have no future. Not one that you want. That your parents would want for you. There's no marriage or children on the cards for me. I refuse to take the risk of passing it on. I refuse to let you watch me die!'

The look on his face was horrible, and she couldn't bear to see it. The shock…the disbelief.

Jess ran for her bedroom, slamming the door behind her. She didn't know if he would come after her, or if he was still sitting at her dinner table, staring at her empty chair in shock. All she knew was that her heart was hurting and she couldn't stop crying, that the pain in her heart was much too real.

This was what she'd wanted to avoid. This was what she had feared would happen if she got close to someone. And, despite all her attempts to stop it, it had happened anyway. She had got close to Adam. Cared for him. Loved him. And now she'd had to devastate him.

It was like learning about having the disease all over again. Grieving again. How many times could she do this? This was why she had to go. This was why she had to leave Thorney and keep herself to herself. Otherwise how many people would she hurt?

She had hurt Adam, destroying his dreams for the two of them, tearing down their bubble and exposing her life for what it truly was...

At that thought, she heard thunder rumbling in the distance. She closed her eyes to stop the sting of tears and sobbed quietly to herself.

She'd done it. She'd told him. About the Huntington's and what that meant. He was a doctor. He'd understand and, if he had any sense about him, he'd realise how serious it was and respect her decision. He'd just remain her colleague and her friend and keep his distance. Understand her decision to leave. He would realise the truth and let her go.

Only she would truly know how much her heart had broken.

He had given her a glimpse of what it

would have like to be with him and now all that had been taken away.

Life wasn't fair.

Love would never be all fluff and kittens and rainbow sparkles for her.

It would be pain and misery and above all loneliness.

It was all she could expect.

CHAPTER THIRTEEN

ADAM WAS STUNNED into silence, into stillness. He'd watched her run from the table to her room and although he'd known he ought to go after her his legs simply hadn't moved. It was as if he'd taken root, her revelation pinning him to the spot.

Huntington's disease... A disorder that caused brain cells to die. An inherited condition that was always fatal. As it progressed it could cause difficulties with memory, depression, clumsiness, jerky movements, problems swallowing, talking or even breathing...

Jerky movements...

His mind flashed back to the lipoma removal and how Jess had reacted. The look of horror on her face.

Now he knew why.

His father must have known. Maybe his mother, too. And no one had thought to tell him. A wave of anger passed over him and he had to let out a slow, steady breath to make himself think about it rationally.

Somehow he managed to stand, his legs now working. He could hear her crying, sobbing, in her room, and the sound of it broke his heart. He needed to talk to her! She was upset…she shouldn't be on her own right now.

His mind was in turmoil. Huntington's! An awful, disabling condition. Poor Jess! And her father had committed suicide! He couldn't imagine the trauma that she had been through, and she had come out of it smiling, bright, happy, determined to bring sunshine into other people's lives, knowing that her own held suffering and upset.

He needed to talk to her. Needed to think. If he let her believe that it was all over for them, then he would lose the second woman he had ever loved. He'd lost Anoush in a hail of bullets, her life snapped out of existence in a second, but Jess?

No future was guaranteed for anyone. Life could be taken at a moment's notice. What mattered was enjoying the time that you did have. Enjoying the present. Because it was a gift. And what was more important than life?

Than love? He loved Jess and he couldn't let her be alone, thinking she'd destroyed their chance at happiness, because she *hadn't*.

He slowed as he came to a realisation.

The Huntington's didn't matter.

What mattered was Jess. His love for Jess and the fact that, even though she didn't think so, he believed they had a life to live together. A present. A future. No matter how uncertain. One more day with her—one week, one month, one year—was better than nothing at all.

He knew what it was like to live without love and it was horrible. Now he'd found it again he was damned sure he wasn't going to give it up without a fight.

Jess sat on her bed, utterly numb. She'd run out of tears, but grief still sat like a giant knot in the centre of her gut.

Adam knew everything now and it had not gone the way she had hoped. She'd wanted to tell him in calm, measured tones, to be un-emotional, but she'd not factored in just how much she felt for him. She'd not been able to sit there, listening to him declaring that he was falling in love with her, when she knew it was already too late for them!

He'd had to know what he was letting himself in for, and now that he did she had no doubt that he would give her a wide berth romantically. He might knock on her door, whisper in soft tones that he was sorry before leaving, but he wouldn't say anything else. Do anything else. What could he say? He would hardly drop to his knees and propose, would he? Not after that.

Sighing, she got to her feet and stripped off her dress and the constricting underwear she'd put on to make the dress look good on her figure. She got into her comfy pyjamas and bathrobe, used some wet wipes to clean her face of make-up and tearstains. But everything she did was done as if in a trance. Numbly. As if she was having an out-of-body experience and was looking down upon herself, or at someone else in a television show.

He'd not come to her door. Hadn't said anything. Had he gone? She wouldn't blame him.

It was so unfair. She'd dreamed of having Adam Campbell fall in love with her! It had been everything she had ever wanted in life—apart from not having an inherited disease—and even though he'd practically handed himself to her on a plate she'd had to knock that plate away and let everything crash to the floor. Let the food spill. The wine stain.

She stared at her sad reflection. There was still work tomorrow, and she'd see Adam there. They'd have to get over the initial awkwardness, but once they did that she felt sure—

A knock on her bedroom door.

Adam.

He was still here.

She hesitated for a minute, not sure she could face him, but…

But if I do it now then I won't have to worry about doing it tomorrow. Just get it over and done with. Accept the pity. Accept the sympathy and the apologies. You know what's coming.

She got up on weary feet and went to open the door.

He stood there, looking at her imploringly. 'We need to talk.'

'Do we? What is there to say?' She brushed past him and led him back to the living room, before standing there, arms crossed defensively. 'What do you want?'

He shook his head, as if in amazement. 'What do I *want*? I want to speak to you about what you just said!'

'What is there to say? I have a life-limiting disease and there is no future for you with me. Nothing. Not the kind that your family wants for you. Not the kind that you deserve.'

'Who says?'

'The disease does.'

'Yeah, well, the disease doesn't get to choose what I decide to do with my life and neither do you!'

He'd raised his voice in frustration and, not sure what to say, she just stared at him. She hadn't expected his anger.

'You say you've got Huntington's... Well, so what? It doesn't matter.'

'It *does* matter.'

'No, it doesn't.'

'You watched the woman you loved die right in front of your eyes and it almost broke you! You think I want you watching me do the exact same thing? Only I won't die in seconds, Adam. I'll die slowly, week after week, month after month, losing a bit of me every day as my brain cells *shrink and die*. I won't put you through it.'

Tears came to her eyes, surprising her. She'd thought she was out of those.

'You don't get to choose what I do with my heart, Jess, *I do*! Yes, losing Anoush was tough! Yes, it almost broke me. But it would break anyone! And I wouldn't change one thing about falling in love with Anoush, even though our time together was so brief. The love was worth it! I'd do it again in a heartbeat. But since meeting you, I've realised I was just existing day by day. *You* made me live again. You made me find joy and happiness. You make me complete and I will take you for as many years as I can get with you! I choose to live my life with you in it, no matter how much time you've got left, because one day with you is preferable to years without you in my life at all!'

The tears dripped down her cheeks and jaw. He was saying some lovely things, but he didn't know how hard it would be!

'You think I haven't seen a Huntington's case?' he asked. 'Well, I have. I know what it can do to someone. And I won't let you go through that alone! I love you, Jess. That's what's important. Love! Let's spend the time we have left together, making each other happy.'

'Oh, Adam! I want to do that—I do. But… The idea of you having to look after me…'

'There are thousands of people looking after their partners in this world. You think they hate it? You think they find it off-putting? That somehow it makes them love *less*? That's dedication. That's love. That's in sickness and in health! You don't get to love someone just when they can walk and talk. You love them for who they are, for who they've been—and you, Jessica Young, are the one person who makes me want to be a better man. Who stands by my side when I need help and when I'm broken. So why can't I do the same thing in return? Do you love me, Jess?'

'You know I do...' she whispered, her breath caught in her throat so it hurt to talk.

'Then be brave. Take my hand and my heart and do with them what you will.' He held out his hand to her. 'Just know that if you take them you can't give them back. They're non-returnable.'

She felt the beginnings of a smile wanting to show itself. He'd said some wonderful things. He'd said all the right things. The only question was, was she brave enough to step into the future with him?

He was brave enough. He'd made that quite clear. And there were no secrets any more. He knew what he was getting into and he still wanted to be with her.

How lucky was she? It looked as if she was getting everything she wanted after all.

Slowly, carefully, she reached out to take his hand in hers and squeezed it tight. 'I'm all yours.'

Adam let out a breath as a big smile broke across his face and he pulled her towards him and kissed her gently on the lips. 'And you're mine. Just know that I will never let you go.'

EPILOGUE

JESS BLEW OUT an exhausted breath, remembering just how much she hated unpacking after a holiday.

No… She smiled. Not a holiday. *A honeymoon.*

She and Adam had had a fabulous time in Mauritius, walking on sandy beaches, sipping cocktails and occasionally practising her very bad schoolgirl French on the poor, unsuspecting locals on those days they'd been out and about in the sunshine.

Though there had been other days when they'd spent hours in bed, enjoying each other's bodies, the French doors open to a view of the clear blue sea.

But, as was always the case after going away, you had to go back to reality. Real life. Unpacking everything. *Laundry.*

Adam's arms slipped around her waist from behind and she felt his lips upon her neck.

'Hey, beautiful. I told you I'd give you a hand with this.'

She loved the feel of his body against hers. The way he fitted her just perfectly. As if they'd been cut from the same mould.

'I wanted to make a start. There's so much to do… We haven't fully unpacked from the move yet, either.'

Adam had told her that he would follow her anywhere, and that if she wanted to pursue her dreams of working in obstetrics then that was what she must do. So, after telling his parents the good news about their relationship, they had told them that they'd be moving to Cardiff whilst Jess did her training.

'But then we'll be right back here, Jack. If you'll still have us?'

'Of course I'll have you back! Don't you forget it!'

Jack and Judy had enveloped them both in a large hug, and Jess had got swept up into the arms of the most loving family she had ever known.

Judy had helped her plan the wedding, which had been held on Thorney, and since then they'd been the best in-laws she could ever have. They'd been so good about her condition—even when Jess had sat down privately with Judy, to apologise because she would never give her the grandchildren she wanted.

'Grandchildren are wonderful—of course they are. But the best gift you could have given me was making my son the happiest he has ever been in his entire life.'

Now clothes were everywhere—even hanging on the wardrobe door, ready to be put away, next to the brand-new suit she'd put out for her first day tomorrow as an obstetrics registrar.

Adam touched the sleeve of the suit, drawing her eye to it. 'Are you nervous?' he asked.

'Yes.'

He turned her to face him and kissed her, smiling. 'Don't be. You'll be amazing. It's your dream! Enjoy it. Soak it all up so that when your training is done we can go back to Thorney and establish your practice there.'

'You don't regret it? Moving away? I know it's your home…'

'My home is where you are. And you're right here. Exactly where you're meant to be.'

Jess wrapped her arms around his neck and

pulled him in for a kiss. 'I love you, Adam. Have I told you that today?'

'I think you might have done, Mrs Campbell. But it never hurts to hear it again.'

'I love you,' she repeated, smiling, staring deeply into his eyes and feeling the strength of his love flow through her, stronger than she could ever have imagined.

'I love you, too,' he said.

And he pressed his lips to hers.

* * * * *